TEMPLE GOLD
TO DIE FOR

BY
WESLEY MARKS

ISBN-13: 978-0-9992673-2-5 paperback
ISBN-13: 978-0-9992673-3-2 e-book

Book layout by www.ebooklaunch.com

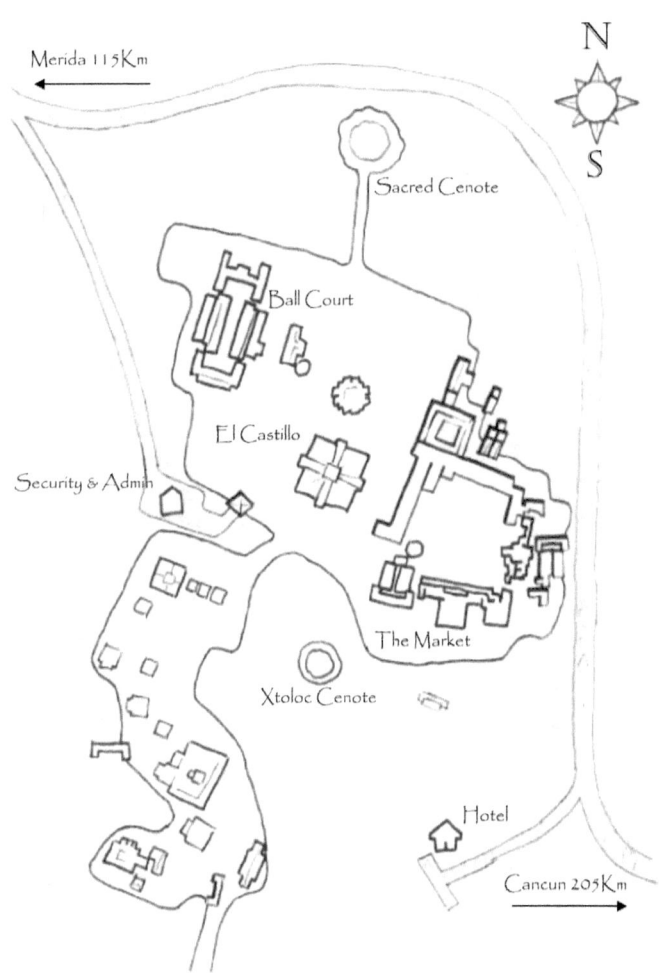

N

S

Merida 115Km

Sacred Cenote

Ball Court

El Castillo

Security & Admin

The Market

Xtoloc Cenote

Hotel

Cancun 205Km

Acknowledgments

My goal is to write things that my students, along with other students, will enjoy reading. That is the reason why with each book I write I invite a small group of my students to read it and to give me feedback. For them it is a chance to understand the writing process and to correct the teacher, but I am very comfortable with that. I want to thank Samantha Ondrick, Long Vu, Alliyah Valencia, and Savanah Gonzalez who took time at the end of their school year to not only read my rough draft but to critique it. Their job was to make certain that it was an enjoyable read and that the characters were believable. They did mark some grammar errors which made it all the more fun for them. They, along with my school librarian Jennifer Hashert, collaborated to help create the final story line that you are about to read. Without their help *Temple God To Die For* would not have a name or the solid characters it has. Thank you.

As always, I have a wonderful editor in Joan Giurdanella who makes certain that everything flows and that it fits within the parameters of the publishing industry. She not only polishes my writing but has become a great encourager and friend. I am deeply grateful to have her working with me.

So please enjoy reading *Temple Gold To Die For* and remember it takes a team to succeed.

Chapter 1

The Goal

"I can't believe that you let two kids, an Indian, and a snail chaser take my treasure!" bellowed Charles Lanning as he read James's report about the discovery and recovery of *El Dorado.* "How could you have let these amateurs get what I have been searching for the last twenty-five years? I have spent millions trying to locate that Spanish shipment, and these boys stumbled across the clues and pieced enough of it together in a few short weeks to find what had been hidden for more than five hundred years. I pay you top dollar to get results, what happened?"

"We thought we were staying a step ahead of them as they found each clue," replied James Farmer. "But the real problem was that in a community of less than a hundred people two new guys stood out like wolves at a sheep convention. When they teamed up with the old Indian, who was from there, everything we did got back to them. We thought we had them by putting a tracking device in one of their backpacks, but the motel owner saw us and called the cops. We might have gotten away with the whole thing had Nick not stepped into the nest of an alligator and been eaten alive."

The head of Mr. Lanning's security team paused, sighing. "It was pure luck that the teenagers stumbled on the clues in the first place. None of your experts came close to what those boys found."

All of this was true, there was no denying it. Any other person would have thrown away the old piece of wood had it not been for that seal stamped on it that looked like the logo for Real Madrid. Their pure innocence kept them doing things that seemed illogical to those who were used to following logic and that made it difficult for James Farmer and his partner, Nick Barnes, to stay ahead of Dalton Miller and Juan Hernandez, the teenage boys who Mr. Lanning now despised.

"Farmer, I am forming a new team to continue searching," declared Mr. Lanning.

"I don't understand. The boys and the Spanish government got the treasure, and we have no clues to where any of the other ships are located. Why would we continue a search without evidence?" asked Farmer.

"What you don't know is that I have had the chance to get copies of the logbook from *El Dorado*, which the boys found. As my experts looked over it, they found some clues that might lead us to the original source of the treasure. If we can track that down, then we stand a chance of finding any remaining treasure." Lanning pulled out the translations of the log and pointed to a line that read, "We waited for the last of the gold and jewels to arrive from the temple where Pedro Alonso Niño had captured both treasure and slaves. Niño's men spoke of a great temple complex and community with tall structures like mountains."

"I know that doesn't seem like much because there are a number of temples that are like mountains, but I read that there is a museum in Santo Domingo that has logbooks and diaries from this time period. I am sending a group to research and see if they can find clues. Go to Santo Domingo with them to continue directing the search, and do everything necessary to find the temple and stop anyone from getting there before us," Mr. Lanning commanded Farmer.

Walking out of Charles Lanning's office, which could have been a museum of stolen art from around the world, James Farmer began to ponder his situation. He had willingly gone to Florida on what he thought was a wild goose chase, but he seemed less comfortable going on this hunt. After being chewed out by his boss for failing him, he reflected on what happened. His partner, Nick Barnes, had been eaten by an alligator and then he was arrested, though in the end he had grown fond of Dalton and Juan, while the sheriff forced him to remain in Florida. While staying in the same motel, he visited with them every day and kept up with the excavation of the treasure ship. By the time he was able to go back to Boston, the three had built an unlikely friendship. Now looking at extending the hunt from Florida to the Dominican Republic and then into Mexico, Farmer wondered who should really get the credit for this find.

Putting those thoughts aside, Farmer returned to his office, gathered the staff that had been assigned to him, and briefed them on their objective. Looking around the room, he saw three large rough-looking men whom Mr. Lanning had hired as bodyguards/investigators with military training, but questionable records. They each had worked in foreign countries fighting for or against the government depending upon who paid the most. It was obvious they were used to violence and in his mind that made controlling them difficult. Mario Bertolli seemed to be the smartest of the three at six feet tall and two hundred pounds, his dark eyes and black hair made him a menacing figure, even without the scar on his right cheek from a knife fight as a kid. Franklin Washington was a little shorter than Mario. But he grew up on the streets of Chicago as a street boxer, so his bulging muscles under his dress shirt stood out. Earl Rodgers was physically the most intimidating of the three. At six-foot-four and pushing three hundred pounds, he was more like a mountain than a man. He had walked onto the University of Tennessee football team as a defensive lineman, but was cut after a year because he lacked the brains or the disciple to play at that level. Frustrated, he joined the army like the other two and found his niche with guns and hand-to-hand combat. The biggest problem with these three was that they could not go anywhere without being noticed, whether alone or together. That is where the fourth member of the team came in. She was a short woman at five-foot-two who carried herself with confidence and intelligence. With a doctorate in archaeology from the University of Miami, Jacqueline Montavilla had proved her worth multiple times as a great researcher. Though she barely reached the shoulder of these four men, she was not intimidated by them in the least. In fact, she was the one who demanded attention in the group. It was not just her education but her superior air.

She seemed to act as if she owned everything and everyone who came into her presence. And even if you were not dazzled by her exotic looks, you were moved by her directness.

James Farmer laid out the plan to go to the Dominican Republic and begin research. Dr. Montavilla would lead that phase while everyone else helped and provided protection or intimidation. Farmer booked separate flights for the team members to keep down suspicion: one for the three bodyguards and another one for him and the archaeologist. To the world, Farmer and Dr. Montavilla would be just a couple spending an extended vacation in the Caribbean. Everyone was to meet in Farmer's suite in Santo Domingo in three days. Lanning's team left the meeting to pack and to catch flights. Farmer finished up some business in his office but took the time to send out a single e-mail before he closed down his computer and went back to his apartment to pack.

Chapter 2

Back at School

When Dalton and Juan showed up at school in the fall, nothing was the same. It was not just that they were entering high school, it was because everyone knew who they were from their great discovery. All of the teachers called them by name, and most of the students, especially the seniors, were aware of what they had found during the summer. Even living in a big city like Dallas, news still travels fast when there is treasure, intrigue, and death involved. The two teenagers couldn't go down the hall without someone stopping to meet them or jokingly asking for a loan. This was definitely not what most freshmen experienced. Most found themselves lost in the crowd, almost nonexistent to all except their close friends, but Juan and Dalton were celebrities it seemed. They had been hounded by people from the time they discovered *El Dorado*, especially by news reporters covering the story. Returning home, they had hoped that things would settle down, but that didn't seem possible now.

Luckily, they had a couple of classes together throughout the day and then soccer practices every afternoon. It seemed like everyone else wanted something from them so they often withdrew from the other students just to get some peace. Their experiences had matured them more than most teenagers their age. They no longer acted like the world revolved around them; they saw things from a perspective that most kids would not get until they were in their thirties. Their soccer teammates were the exception, since they had played with them for a while. They were the only students who treated them as equals and brothers, not as celebrities. That changed with a chance meeting in the hallway.

While the boys were in middle school, they had been more focused on soccer and barely noticed girls. Oh, they talked about them all the time, but they were shy and awkward at that age and having a girlfriend just didn't seem to be important. Now that they were in high school, it seemed that there were a lot more girls around or at least they noticed more girls. One sophomore girl noticed Dalton, and he, in turn, noticed her back. In the library while he was looking at a history book, he saw a dark-haired girl with dimples and green eyes looking up from her table of friends and smile at him. Their eyes met at the exact same time, and he smiled back. He felt as if the air just escaped out of him as he gazed into emerald eyes. His knees became a little shaky as he smiled back, realizing that she was smiling at only him. Being a year older, he didn't know her name, nor did he have any classes with her, but he felt a connection that began to haunt him.

"Juan, have you ever had that weird feeling when you saw a girl?" asked Dalton.

"You mean that disgusting feeling when you see she has a big nose with a booger hanging out of it?" laughed Juan.

Reaching over and hitting Juan on the shoulder, he snorted, "No, that feeling that you don't know this girl, but you want to get to know her, dummy."

"Oh, that feeling. No, except when I look at Selena Gomez, she is hot," drooled Juan.

"I'm talking about someone who is real and our age, not some star you will never meet," sighed Dalton. "Well, there is a girl I saw in the library today who was beautiful, and she smiled at me. Do you think she was just being nice or she wanted to meet me?"

"How do I know? What's her name?"

"If I knew her name, I would probably already know her. Can you help me find out who she is?" asked Dalton.

"If you're sure she's a sophomore, then we can just look in last year's yearbook for her picture. It's not like we haven't already learned how to find important information after all of the time we spent in the library and on the Internet searching for *El Dorado* this summer," he laughed.

The next day at lunch, Dalton and Juan went to the library and asked the lady at the counter for the previous year's yearbook and spent their whole lunch period looking at pictures until they found the girl. Molly Welsh was the name listed under the photograph, but no other information. "Does this seem like we are stalkers now?" asked Dalton.

"No, but it does feel like you owe me a lunch since now I am starving," Juan replied as he pulled an energy bar out of his backpack.

"What are you complaining about? You are getting fat anyway!" Dalton quipped with a mischievous grin on his face. He quickly jumped back because he knew Juan would be swinging at him for that comment. Which he did.

"Fat! At least I am still faster than you!" Juan laughed.

The boys headed off to class and then off to practice after school. Juan immediately smoked Dalton on the field and then turned around chuckling while backpedaling only to trip on his own feet and fall. Dalton ran up, "Who's laughing now, clumsy," he bantered while reaching down to help Juan up. Both boys grinned and continued playing. While at practice, the boys asked around about Molly and one of the guys on the team knew her and gave Dalton her phone number. Now it was up to him to decide if he was going to call or not.

Being a little shy, he waited a few days and happened to see her in the hallway as he and Juan were walking to class. She saw him and smiled again. Juan said, "So that is Molly. Go introduce yourself."

"I can't. I would be too embarrassed to just walk up and say something," Dalton shyly replied.

Being much more confident, Juan walked across to where Molly was and introduced himself. "Hi, I am Juan Hernandez and you are Molly Welsh, right?"

Smiling, she replied, "Yes, but how did you know my name?"

"That's a story for Dalton to tell you. Dalton, come over and meet my new friend, Molly," Juan hollered. Smiling like he had just told the best joke in the world.

Dalton walked over said, "Hi, I'm Dalton." He kept his voice low and looked down to avoid eye contact.

"I know who both of you are, you are kind of famous around here," said Molly. "Juan said you have a story to tell me." Molly replied.

Giving Juan that "I'm going to kill you look," Dalton confessed to stalking her after the smile in the library and getting her phone number from one of his soccer teammates.

"You have my phone number? Then why didn't you just text me?" Molly asked with a grin on her face.

"To be honest, I was scared that you had just smiled at me like you might smile at anyone else. I didn't want to seem weird. If it hadn't been for macho man here," Dalton said, pointing to Juan, "I probably still would not have spoken to you."

"I am glad you did. I did smile at you on purpose. I just didn't want to seem like all of the other people who were probably coming up to you to get to know you because of the treasure," said Molly. "Though I am very interested in hearing the whole story."

"I have to go now, otherwise I will be late to geometry, and Ms. Jones does not tolerate tardiness. I have soccer practice after school, can we meet then?" Dalton asked.

"I need to get to chemistry myself. Call me when you are finished and I should be finished with choir," she said as she hurried off in the other direction. Dalton watched her the whole way.

"Dude, you are pathetic," laughed Juan.

"Maybe so, but I don't see you making plans with a girl," Dalton hollered as he ran down the hall to Mr. Jones's class.

That afternoon when practice was over, he called Molly and they met at the McDonald's down the street from the school. Sitting in a booth facing the door, he waited. His hands were sweaty, even though he showered after soccer practice. He had never met a girl anyplace by himself. Once, he had gone to the movies with a group of friends that included girls, but never by himself, so he was nervous, with all kinds of thoughts running through his mind. *What if she doesn't like me? What if she just wants to know me because of the treasure? What if I say something stupid or spill a drink on her?* he questioned in his mind. These thoughts did not calm him in the least, but instead made him even more nervous. *I have got to stop thinking and just relax,* he said quietly to himself. Just as he got the words out, she walked through the door. The sun behind her head made her hair seem to shine and give her an angelic look. The sight made him choke on the word *hello* as he tried to say it out loud. Smiling, she waved and walked over to the booth.

"Have you been waiting long? I had to stay a few more minutes to finish filing away the music we were working on in choir."

"No, I just walked in a few minutes ago. Can I get you something to drink?" he politely asked.

"Sure, a Coke would be great," she said as he got up to go to the counter.

Returning with two Cokes in his hands, he offered one to her with a smile and then sat down in the booth across from her. Starting a conversation with someone you don't know, but would like to get to know, was difficult. But after a few quiet moments, he asked, "What were you singing in choir?"

Her eyes lit up because he wanted to talk about her. "We are working on a piece in Latin for a contest next month. I struggle enough singing the words much less remembering the title," she laughed.

"I would be out of luck if I had to sing in another language. I started Spanish this semester and I can't remember a word of it. Thank goodness for Juan. He tries to help me, but most of the time I just don't get it."

"Singing in Latin is not that hard. You just sing what is on the paper but don't understand a word of it."

"I would be afraid that they would have me singing an acceptance into military school or something," chuckled Dalton.

"What is it you like to do?"

"I love to play soccer. That is how Juan and I met. When we moved here the realtor suggested a soccer team that her son had played on. I went to practice and Juan and I collided on the pitch and have been best friends ever since. We do just about everything together," informed Dalton. "That is the reason we discovered *El Dorado*. He went with me to Florida while my dad did some work."

"Since you brought it up, can I ask you about the treasure?" she sheepishly asked.

"Sure. As I said, Juan and I were in Florida on a small island kayaking when we found a piece of wood. The wood had a symbol that looked like a soccer logo and it turned out to be Queen Isabella's seal from 1501. After more research and finding another piece of wood, we discovered it was a barrel that was from a ship at a time before Europeans had been in America yet. We did a lot of research online and in the University of Miami's libraries and determined it had to have been a ship blown off course from a large fleet of ships lost in a hurricane in 1502. When we continued our search in the water, we found the barrel that contained the diary of Captain Antonio de Torres and *El Dorado*'s logbook. The ship was carrying gold back to Spain and it, along with twenty-six other ships, was lost. Researching the land with Google Earth, we were able to find several areas in the swamp that were not flat, so we started looking into them and found the ship. In the process, we were being watched by two men who followed us into the swamp. And when they tried to take the treasure, one of them was eaten by an alligator. Spain and SMU now have the treasure because they paid to have it all excavated, but we got all the credit for finding it. I could take to you SMU sometime to see it if you want. They allow me to visit any time I want. In fact, they kind of treat us like kings around there. It's kind of fun.

"I would love to. I haven't been to SMU so between that and the exhibit it would be fun." Her phone rang, and it was her mother calling to pick her up on her way home from work. Molly thanked Dalton for the Coke and the visit and asked if they could hang out again. He eagerly agreed.

Chapter 3

The E-Mail

J uan went home when practice was over. After finishing his homework, he opened up his computer to check to see if there were any assignments he missed on Google classroom. He also logged into his e-mail and found an unusual message. It had come from an account he did not know and was titled, "Before *El Dorado*." That seemed like a strange e-mail. But he opened it and found that someone had written him about Mr. Lanning's men discovering more in Antonio de Torres's diary. The writer thought it provided clues that might lead to the original source of the gold. The e-mail said that some people were going to Santo Domingo to search the records to see if they could find any information on a Pedro Alonso Niño, whose men had loaded the gold onto the ships. The last sentence of the e-mail was a little puzzling:

> I did not mean to Bug you, but I thought this might Eat you up if you did not know about it, especially as Swamped as you are.
>
> Nick

"I don't know a Nick. Who was Pedro Alonso Niño? And what is this weird message at the end mean?" All of these things confused Juan, but he knew Dalton could help him unravel this mystery.

Juan dialed Dalton's number immediately. "Dalton, you home yet from your date?" teased Juan.

"It was not a date, we just met for a Coke."

"Did you meet her by yourself, talk, and share a drink?" questioned Juan.

"Yes!"

"Then it was a date, even if you didn't kiss her," Juan laughed.

"Okay, it was a date. I had a great time visiting with her. She sings Latin in the choir. We even talked about you and how we met. She did ask about *El Dorado* like you thought she would, but she just wanted to hear the story, nothing else," Dalton said.

"Speaking of *El Dorado*, I got a weird e-mail today. Have you opened your e-mail to see if you got it also?" Juan asked.

"No, but I will do it now," he said, going to his computer and logging on. "Are you talking about the e-mail with the before *El Dorado* subject line?"

"Yes. Take a minute and read it," responded Juan, which Dalton did.

"What do you think?" Juan questioned.

"It's weird. This person Nick says that Mr. Lanning is trying to find where the gold came from. Who's Nick?" Dalton asked.

"That's the first mystery and what does the last sentence mean?"

Dalton, contemplating the sentence for a minute. "There are odd words capitalized: *Bug*, *Eat*, *Swamp*, and *Nick*. What do they mean? Did we eat a bug in the swamp with Nick? Wait a minute. Nick was the name of the guy who was following us. He was eaten in the swamp, but I don't get the word *bug*?"

Juan replied, "Nick was the guy who put the bug in my backpack to track us! But it can't be a message from him, we saw him eaten by an alligator. If it is not from him, then it could only be from James Farmer."

"We did get to know him while he waited. It turned out he was a really nice guy. Doesn't he still work for Mr. Lanning?" Dalton asked.

"Last time I heard. But why would he be telling us this?" Juan wondered out loud.

"The only thing I can think is that he doesn't like what Mr. Lanning is up to and he knew that we now have connections to find the answers first," Dalton said while responding to the e-mail. "I am going to write him back to make certain what we think and will send you a copy. Call you back in a few minutes." Then he hung up the phone and began typing away at the keyboard.

Dear Nick,

Sorry that this is eating you up. Never been to Santo Domingo, but you are right in saying Pedro Alonso Niño has. I heard he was a farmer before a conquistador. Thank you for the heads up, keep yours down."

Sincerely,

The Snail

He sent a copy to Juan along with his response and as soon as he hit send he called Juan back. "What do you think about my response?

"I think if it is Farmer he will know we know and are curious. If not, it should confuse the sender," Juan said.

"That was my thought, too. Now what do we do with this information?" asked Dalton.

"I will research Pedro Alonso Niño and you go get your dad. Let's see what he thinks."

Dalton set his phone down and went into the living room where his father was sitting in a comfortable chair reading a book. He barely saw Dalton walk in because the only light in the room was the reading lamp next to his chair. When Dalton spoke, Dr. Miller jumped in surprise. "Dad, can you come into my room for a minute?"

With his heart pounding from being startled, Dalton's dad put down his book with a marker on the last page he read and got up to walk into his son's bedroom. "What's going on, Dalton?"

"Juan and I received an e-mail and we want you to look at it," Dalton said while leading him over to his computer. "Read it and then tell Juan and me what you think."

Seeing the phone on the desk he called out, "Hello, Juan. How are you doing?"

"Fine, Dr. Miller. How are the snails breeding?" Juan laughed, making fun of the reason they had originally gone to Florida.

"Slowly" was the typical reply Juan would get from Dr. Miller with a short laugh. Dr. Miller bent down to the computer screen and read. "This e-mail is strange. What do you guys think about it?"

"Well, we think it is from James Farmer because he is the only one who knew all of the details that were highlighted in the e-mail," Dalton said.

"I think you are right. But why do you think he felt it necessary to contact you guys about continued research on *El Dorado*?" queried Dr. Miller.

"That is what we are wondering," replied Juan. "We think maybe Mr. Lanning is up to his old tricks of trying to find artifacts and keeping them for himself or selling them on the black market. Farmer still works for Mr. Lanning, but I think he has decided that what is going on is not right. We are probably the only ones who have ever beaten Lanning and who understands what he really wants, so he reached out to us."

"That is true. But what can we do at this point?" Dr. Miller asked.

"I sent him an e-mail that was coded, letting him know we thought it was him and telling him to keep his head down. I figured he would understand and not reply unless he found anything else out," said Dalton.

"Good response. Let me contact Dr. Frances Weston, head of archaeology at SMU and see what she thinks. I will also contact Howard Swartz, who's in charge of security for SMU, just in case. Forward me the e-mail and I will send it to them along with your thoughts," said Dr. Miller.

The next day, after reading the e-mails, Dr. Weston called Dr. Miller to set up a meeting with him, the boys, and Mr. Swartz. Dr. Miller texted both boys and told him he would pick them up after practice.

When Dr. Miller, Dalton, and Juan arrived at SMU, Dr. Weston wasted no time discussing the page she had studied from *El Dorado*'s log.

"Thank you for coming. I figured since James Farmer has taken the time to e-mail that it meant that it was important. They may be onto something with this clue. We didn't notice it while we were going over the text, because we were focused on the treasure not its source. The question that I think we need to discuss is: Do we pursue it or let Mr. Lanning try to find the origin of the treasure?" Dr. Weston asked.

Dalton spoke up first. After all that had happened over the last four months, he felt comfortable speaking his mind to Dr. Weston and Mr. Swartz. In fact, everyone associated with *El Dorado* learned quickly that both young men had good ideas and deserved to be heard. "I don't think that James Farmer would have written to us had he thought what Mr. Lanning was up to any good. He is risking his job to let us know and he is trying to do it in a way that will not be understood by other people. I read this as a plea for us to find it before Lanning."

"As much as I don't want to get involved in anything associated with Mr. Lanning again, I think you are right, Dalton," Dr. Miller said. "Farmer proved to be a friend after all that took place in Florida. Mr. Swartz, as head of security, you spent time with him, what do you think?"

"I agree," said Mr. Swartz. "Farmer turned out to be a good man, just doing his job. The way he interacted with all of us and especially the boys the couple of weeks he was forced to stay proved he was not only reliable, but trustworthy. I agree with Dalton, there is something important there and he feels that if we don't act then whatever is found will be lost."

"So, I think we are all agreed that there is a need, but how are we going to find the answers?" asked Juan.

"We have to go to Santo Domingo. I know we're in school, but there must be a way that we can miss going to class and work out something with our teachers. Then we can come back and play soccer in the spring," blurted out Dalton.

"I don't think so," said Dr. Miller. "It was dangerous enough the last time, no telling how dangerous this could be. We now know that Mr. Lanning will stop at nothing to find his treasure. I can't allow you to be exposed to the danger."

"Dad, we started this and we want to finish it. You are always saying 'finish what you started,' so let us finish it," Dalton begged and Juan agreed.

"You know I want you to finish what you start, but this is different and dangerous."

Dr. Weston had waited quietly, not wanting to get between a father and son, but she had an idea. "The first part of this project is pure research and should be done by someone who not only is good at research, which you boys have become, but can read the language fluently. One of my doctoral students is fluent in Spanish and has been working on Aztec and Mayan archaeology. She would be the ideal person to have go to Santo Domingo and research for us. On top of that, no one would know her, so she would be able to work freely. Mr. Swartz can we figure out some kind of protection for her as she researches, maybe a research assistant who is also a bodyguard?"

"I think I can find someone who might be able to do that. Give me a day and I will have someone here," Mr. Swartz replied.

The boys were visibly upset that they were being left out. Dr. Weston realized she owed Dalton and Juan for all of the notoriety and fame they had brought to SMU. "Here is the deal I will make with you boys: Let my student go and do the groundwork, and I will personally make certain that you are involved in everything she finds. You will be included in all correspondence and we will value your input. If we are still working in Santo Domingo during your Thanksgiving break, we will fly you out to be hands on, if that is okay with your father."

Everyone agreed. The boys really had no choice, and Dr. Miller thought this would come to nothing. Before they left, Dr. Weston called his graduate student Mercedes Benavides and asked her to come to her office right away. When she arrived, Dr. Weston introduced her to the group. Mercedes was thrilled to meet Dalton and Juan and talk to them about their discovery.

"We feel like we need to continue the search in the name of science," said Dr. Weston. "We don't want black market profiteers like Charles Lanning to ruin our chances of understanding history. What is your feeling on the subject, Ms. Benavides?"

"History needs to be preserved and studied," replied Mercedes. "When things move into private collections or when untrained people collect items, they destroy our ability to learn."

"Good. We would like for you to go to Santo Domingo to research this Pedro Alonso Niño and see if you can find any logs, notes, or any other information that can lead us to the source of the treasure on *El Dorado*. There is one major complication: Another team is already there, so you must work quickly and quietly. In the past, Mr. Lanning's team has been willing to resort to violence. Because of that, Mr. Swartz will provide a security person who will travel with you and act as your research assistant. Are you interested in this project?" Dr. Weston asked.

"Absolutely! When do you want me to go?"

"I would like for you to leave as soon as possible. I will contact your doctoral supervisor and assign someone else to the class you are teaching. You will need to send daily reports—even if they are short—to me and please include both Dalton and Juan. I will make all of the travel arrangements for you."

"Thank you for this opportunity, I feel very honored. I should go now to pack and get notes together for my class. Let me know when I will be traveling and I will be ready," Mercedes said as she shook hands with everyone and walked out of the door.

"That is settled and now we hope for the best," Dr. Miller said, and then gave a sigh of relief.

Chapter 4

Creating the Team

G oing back to school the next day was hard for Dalton and Juan. They wanted to be on their way to Santo Domingo, but that was not an option. Mercedes Benavides was more qualified to do the research than they were and had the background to understand the material, but that did not help pacify either of the boys. It was their mystery to solve. They were the ones to find *El Dorado,* and James Farmer had contacted them. But what choice did they have? They were just kids.

It was the phrase that bothered them the most. "They were just kids" who found hundreds of millions of dollars worth of gold and jewels ... who figured out all of the clues to find a five-hundred-year old shipwreck ... and who were able to create a plan to disguise what they were doing so trained men would get lost.

"We should be going, but that's not going to happen. Hopefully, Mercedes will keep us in the loop, at least then we will feel a part of this adventure," Dalton said to Juan.

Dalton hung around Molly's locker before geometry. Sure enough, she stopped there and was pleased to see him. "Are you stalking me?" she asked with a grin.

Too shy to look her in the face, he replied, "I don't know if I would call it stalking, but I hoped I might see you on your way to chemistry."

"To be honest I was hoping you would. I enjoyed the Coke the other day, but then I didn't see you or hear from you yesterday, so I was afraid that maybe you weren't interested anymore."

"I'm so sorry. I didn't want to seem pushy so I didn't call you. When I got home, Juan and I had received an e-mail about *El Dorado*. That caused us to have to go to SMU for a meeting."

"You are still working on your find?" she asked, confused.

"Not exactly. All of the excavation and cataloging have been completed, so the work on *El Dorado* itself is finished. Other than some museum openings about the treasure around Christmas in Spain and then at SMU in January, we are done."

Dalton then explained to Molly that the people who tried to take the treasure from the boys were now trying to find its source. So, the head of the archaeology department at SMU decided that their team should work on finding it before the bad guys, in case there is any more treasure or artifacts. Dr. Weston didn't want "history" being sold on the black market, so it was important that the SMU team found the source first.

"It's funny," Dalton told Molly. "Ten months ago, I could have cared less what was in a museum or what someone owned. I liked history but did not love it. Now all that has changed. To be a part of finding unsolved history has gotten into my blood, kind of like Indiana Jones, without the hat or the whip."

"That must be exciting," said Molly. "Are you going back to Florida to hunt then?"

"No. A research team from the university is leaving soon for Santo Domingo in the Dominican Republic to see if they can track down any clues. Our parents and the university won't let us go because they're afraid it might be dangerous. The other team will do anything to find the source. Dr. Weston told us that if they were still researching at Thanksgiving break then we might be allowed to go," replied Dalton, feeling a little dejected.

"I have to go to chemistry, but a couple of friends and I are going to the mall after school. Do you and Juan want to meet us there?" Molly asked.

"We have practice, but after that we'll be there," he answered, with his heart beating so loud he thought she might hear it. Both headed off quickly to class so neither would be late.

Juan saw Dalton walk into class just as the bell was ringing and quickly slip into his seat. Mrs. Jones gave him a stern look, but she let it slide. After class started, he quietly told Juan that they were going to the mall after practice. With a funny smile on his face, Juan nodded OK. He guessed that Molly was involved since both of them hated to go to the mall, except to see a movie.

Juan expected to be a third wheel at the mall, not knowing that Molly had invited some friends to go who were cute and friendly. They spent a couple of hours walking around talking and looking at all kinds of stuff. They even stopped to get a cookie and drink so Juan enjoyed himself. Dalton was definitely having a good time being with Molly.

Late morning that same day, Mercedes Benavides had received a phone call from Mr. Swartz asking her to come by his office. Upon arrival she saw a tall, nice-looking black man standing bent over the desk looking at a map. He looked up just as she walked in and a pleasant smile crossed his face. "This is Desmond White. He will be your assistant and provide security for you," said Mr. Swartz, nodding toward Mr. White.

"Encantada en cononcerle, Señorita Benavides," he said while reaching out his large hand to shake.

Taken back by being formally greeted in Spanish, Mercedes replied, "It is nice to meet you also, Mr. White."

With a grin on his face, "I know, you didn't expect me to speak Spanish. I found out in the service that I have a knack for languages. I also speak German, Russian, and Mandarin, but I hope we will not run into anyone from those countries in the Dominican Republic," he laughed.

"Mr. White is a former SEAL who has worked on several continents providing security and classified work for the U.S. Navy. After mustering out, he decided to go back to school and happens to be a student here. We met when one of his former officers asked me to see if he could work in security on campus. I would have told you about him yesterday, but I did not want to presume he would be able to leave class for an extended period of time without checking. It seems a call from the president of the university to his professors seemed to clear his schedule and even allow him to do some of his work while he is gone so he will not get behind. He has generously agreed to go with you. Desmond is not only good with languages, but with technology and research, so he is also there to help you, not just walk around like some massive bodyguard. Though with his size he would do that well," said Mr. Swartz, laughing.

They visited for a few minutes, talking about security and what might be expected considering what Mr. Swartz had seen in Florida from James Farmer and his employer, Charles Lanning. Dr. Weston had booked them a late flight that evening through Miami and on into Santo Domingo. Their reservations included rooms at Hotel Palacio on Calle Duarte 106 in the Colonial Zone. It was close to several of the museums where they would be conducting research. Their flights left at seven so each went home to finish packing and a car picked them to take them to Dallas-Fort Worth airport for their flight.

It was uncomfortable at first as the two sat waiting for their flight to leave. Neither knew much about the other and for the next few weeks they would be spending almost every moment together.

"I thought when I got out of the service and went back to school that I would not be going out on a mission again," Desmond commented. "Mr. Swartz gave me some background on *El Dorado* and a little of who we are up against. What can you tell me about all of this?"

"*El Dorado* was a Spanish ship leading an armada of thirty-two small ships back to Spain loaded with treasure that had been found. After leaving Santo Domingo, a hurricane sunk twenty-seven of the ships, including *El Dorado*. The others barely made it to islands where they were found safe. The Spanish authorities thought they all sunk in the Caribbean until two teenage boys discovered one of them this summer in Florida. Others had been looking for them as well and particularly Charles Lanning who tried to steal it from the boys. One of those men is the one the boys believe contacted them about this new effort. Two men were working for Mr. Lanning; unfortunately, one was eaten by an alligator in front of all of them and the other was arrested by the sheriff. Turned out he was a nice guy, and they became acquainted and even built a friendship. His name is James Farmer and the coded message the boys received could have only come from him. Now Mr. Lanning's team is searching for the origin of the treasure, and Dr. Weston and I both agree that if they get to it first then it will be lost to the black market."

"So, let me get this straight, all of this is hinged on two boys?" Desmond replied in complete surprise.

"Yes. I met Dalton and Juan yesterday for the first time. I read a lot about their find and meeting them they seem like just ordinary kids, but they are very clever. They wanted to come along, but Dr. Weston and Dr. Miller, Dalton's father, would not allow them to miss school. The two teenagers, guided by Dr. Miller, a professor at the university, did the research on *El Dorado* and put the clues together to find it. Their research and assumptions proved to be equal to many well-seasoned researchers, so don't discount them because of their age. We are to send reports to Dr. Weston and each of the boys. That was the compromise they came up with, but it was also a move by Dr. Weston to keep the boys' minds working on the project. I'm sure you will get to meet them before we are through with this," she said while keeping an eye on the time for their departure. Mercedes, reached into her backpack and pulled out a folder with the boys' pictures.

"How old are these kids?"

"Fourteen and just starting high school," she replied.

"When I was just starting high school, I was interested in football and girls, not researching and treasure."

"I think they just stumbled on to their love of history and research, but the rest is probably true with them, though soccer seems to be their sport. When I met them, they both were wearing jackets from professional soccer teams."

"You said they received information from someone they thought was James Farmer," said Desmond. "How do they know it was from him?"

"Dr. Weston said that the clues in the e-mail pointed to the dead partner of Farmer, using information that only he and a few others would have known. Farmer is still working for Mr. Lanning, so with all of the facts they are certain that this former adversary is now trying to help them."

"If that is true, we can use that to our advantage. Can the boys contact him again?" Desmond asked.

"Yes, they already have. Why?"

"If we can open a channel of communications with him, then we can know what they are doing and where. We could stay one step ahead of them, out of their way and maybe even narrow your search?"

Mercedes, thinking about the endless directions the research could take them, agreed and before they boarded the plane e-mailed the boys with that thought.

On the plane, they decided that they would travel as a couple, with her researching for her doctorate and him just coming along to keep her company. That would give him the ability to move around more and the excuse of why they would be together all the time. Their hotel room was a suite with adjoining rooms and a living room that would be used as their research center. The rest of the flight they chatted about their backgrounds and likes, but most of all they got to know each other better.

Desmond and Mercedes grabbed dinner in Miami while they waited for their next flight. Mr. Swartz had arranged a rental car with GPS to be waiting for them at the airport so they could get around the island. Leaving the car rental kiosk, Desmond turned left out of the airport on to Autopista Los Americas, which ran along the coastline to Santo Domingo. Twenty-five minutes later, he got off the highway onto Calle Duarte, heading toward the Colonial Zone, and ten blocks later they arrived at Hotel Palacio.

As Desmond pulled up to the pinkish hotel, a bellhop came out to collect their bags and a valet parked their car in the rear of the building. Mercedes walked up to the large black front desk and spoke to the young lady who was the night manager for the hotel. "I am Mercedes Benavides and I have a suite reserved for Mr. White and me."

"Yes, Ms. Benavides, your rooms are ready. I have an arrival date, but I do not have a departure date for you."

"I am here doing research for my PhD, so I am not sure if we will be here a week, or a month yet. You should have a note that the university is paying for all of our expenses while we are here," Mercedes replied.

"Yes, I see that note now. Please let us know if there is anything you require and our staff will happily help you. I have sent your luggage up to your rooms, and the bellman should be there waiting to show you around and make sure everything is to your liking," the manager replied.

Mercedes thanked her then turned and found Desmond looking at a rack of pamphlets of what to do and where to go. "Find anything interesting?" she inquired.

"I picked up brochures on the museums and other historical sites. I figured that is what we are here for, but they have some beautiful snorkeling and offshore fishing trips if that interests you," he said with a grin.

"It interests me, but first things first. I am tired and our luggage is already headed to the room so I am heading that direction."

He followed her to the elevator and rode to the second floor then turned left to their suite—rooms 206 and 208. The bedrooms had a large living room between them. The bedspreads were the colors of the sunset with reds, oranges, browns, and yellows, and the living room continued the motif of the beauty of the Caribbean and featured black leather couches. All three rooms had ornate lamps, vibrant paintings, and picturesque windows that looked out over a city of six-hundred-year-old structures. Had it not been for the work that they needed to do, this would have been a comfortable, beautiful, and romantic place to spend time.

While they slept, Mr. Lanning's team discussed the day's work. "What kind of progress did you make today, Dr. Montavilla?" asked James Farmer as they entered their own rooms in another hotel in Santo Domingo.

"Nothing major unfortunately. We have established that Pedro Alonso Niño was based out of Santo Domingo, that he did make trips from here to other places in the Caribbean, but nothing to tell us where he went. The only thing we can confirm is that Niño was here. That is at least a start on our first day of research," Dr. Montavilla replied.

Agreeing, Farmer thought about all that was at stake: the potential for new discoveries from the Mayan period, the chance to have a greater understanding of these mysterious people, and not the least the discovery of new artifacts, including treasures from this lost civilization. All of these sounded appealing to him, even though a year ago he had only been interested in doing his job as a security specialist for Charles Lanning. He never thought about history and the things that represent it in his life. Even in school, history was a subject he liked but did not love, now it seemed more alive than ever before. *El Dorado* was not the first historical adventure Mr. Lanning had sent him on; there had been others. Farmer had gone to Argentina to acquire a pot that must have been important, but it was just a simple snatch-and-grab job. He had also traveled to Paris to collect a painting that he thought was ugly, but to his boss it was worth millions. He never cared about where any of it came from or what it meant, he just did as he was told and was well paid for his efforts. In fact, his whole life could have been described in that manner, do well and get paid, but now he felt a passion for the why, how, and when of the history of his assignments. He could attribute that only to two young boys who got excited about a piece of wood and their lust for finding the answers. That passion now burned in him, but with one great dilemma, he worked for the man who cared less about the history and more about the value.

Farmer sat down at his computer to check his e-mails and to work through the problems that he dealt with for Mr. Lanning. After about thirty minutes of directing personnel to do or not do things, he closed out his corporate e-mail and opened a private one. There was the response from the boys. He knew they would figure it out; they were clever young men. The references to Nick Barnes and eaten were obvious and the reference to Niño confirmed that they had understood his message. But now what? He thumbed the mouse over to the reply button and proceeded to tap it.

Dear Snail,

The beaches are beautiful and the museums are even better. It is hard to find a taxi for five though the drivers do their best. Today was just a confirmation of why we enjoy this place, but no idea where we will end up in the future. Hoped that you might crawl out of your shell but speed is difficult for a snail.

Nick

He reread it, knew that the boys would understand the message, and then tapped the send button. Magically, it was transported through cyberspace and delivered. He felt a lightness in his spirit, knowing that what he was doing was the right thing even though he was on the wrong side. He closed his computer, dressed for bed, and then dozed off to the idea of a better outcome in life.

Juan had just finished some English homework he was doing, a research paper on Mark Twain. In the past, he hated to research, now he found he enjoyed it. Finding the things he didn't know and then assembling them into a workable thought or idea, creating from the past what people at the time already understood gave Juan pleasure, and he even excelled in it. Before he turned his computer off for the night, he saw the icon showing a new e-mails. Clicking on the icon, he saw a message and within a few moments understood it. Farmer was in Santo Domingo with four other people and they have started to search. From his description, it appeared that they had not been there long and that they had only established that Pedro Alonso Niño had been in Santo Domingo but nothing else.

He texted Dalton immediately, and Dalton confirmed that he had just received the e-mail and that he agreed with Juan's interpretation. "Now what?" replied Juan.

Dalton called Juan because he had the exact same questions. "Do you think we should talk to Mr. Swartz about this?"

Juan thought about that question for a few minutes. "Mr. Swartz didn't receive this, we did." Juan then reminded Dalton that Farmer trusted them and even though Mr. Swartz had been in Florida with them, Farmer's friendship was with them. So, four other people are with Farmer now, and if one of them is a researcher, then that leaves three others as muscle, the kind that wouldn't hesitate to hurt someone. Then he said, "We didn't get to go, but we are still involved with this project so we need to send this to Mr. Swartz and to Mercedes Benavides and see what they think."

"Right. I will forward the letter to Swartz with our notes on it and will make certain that Mercedes gets a copy," Dalton concluded. "You respond to Farmer."

Each of the boys spent the next twenty minutes doing their part and then headed off to bed knowing that they were doing the right thing. Dalton would tell his father about all of it in the morning.

Chapter 5

Santo Domingo

E ven though Santo Domingo was a typical beautiful Caribbean town, with its laid-back attitude, when Mercedes woke up the next morning she knew she had work to do. She quickly showered and dressed, pulling her long black hair into a ponytail since she was working not going out and then walked over to Desmond bedroom door. She knocked and entered when he responded, finding him just dressed even though he appeared to have been up for a while. Turned out it was his custom to rise early and run three miles every morning, shower, and then dress for the day. Neither of them had looked at their e-mails since the previous night.

"Did you sleep well?" Desmond asked Mercedes as he slipped on his Sperry's and stood to greet her.

"Yes. I was exhausted from the quick trip and late night. I think I went to sleep the minute my hcad hit the pillow. How about you?"

"I sent the e-mail we had talked about to Mr. Swartz seeing if the boys could help us contact this James Farmer. I went quickly off to sleep after that. I'm sure he hasn't had time to answer, so I haven't checked this morning. I thought we might go down and have breakfast, then check e-mails, and begin looking over the museums that you think are going to help us the most," he directed.

"I am hungry, so let's go eat and discuss my research plan," she said, turning toward the door and heading out. He smiled as she led the way out. Compared to all of the missions he had been on before, this was definitely the most attractive of them.

They found a table out in the courtyard that made up the center of the hotel and seated themselves at a round wooden table with a white umbrella towering over them. The area had brick walkways and patios along with flowing bushes and trees set in the raised brick beds. A smiling waitress came and took their drink orders, which both happened to be coffee and left them to look over the menu. After selecting their breakfast, they began to discuss their day.

"I think I want to start at the Museo de las Casas Reales, because they are known to have a history collection on the city itself. I figure if Pedro Alonso Niño came to the city at all we should find him mentioned in the history of the city, especially if he did bring treasure here," informed Mercedes.

Pulling out one of the brochures Desmond had picked up the night before, he found the museum on the map. "It is four blocks up to the right from the hotel. I ran by it this morning and didn't even notice it," chuckled Desmond.

"You have been up running this morning? I guess that makes sense considering your background. I work out, but I'm not awake enough in the morning to run," she laughed. About then, their breakfast arrived and they enjoyed the fruit and eggs, but most of all the conversation about their childhoods, where they grew up, and about their families. Both enjoyed learning about the other and sharing their own past.

They charged the meal to the room and went back up to pick up their things to head to the museum. Both took a few minutes to check their e-mail and were surprised at what they found. Desmond found his reply from Mr. Swartz, who thought it might be a good idea to contact Farmer through the boys. He looked up from the table in the living room where both of them had set up their laptops. She seemed to be looking up with a comment at the same time.

"I got an e-mail," they both said at the same time, with looks of astonishment on their faces.

"Ladies first, please," he responded in a chivalrous manner.

"The boys have received another e-mail from Farmer and they have forwarded it to me along with their interpretation. Read it and tell me what you think," she said sliding the computer around for him to read.

After a few minutes, Desmond said, "I'm not sure I understand the code, but they both seem to understand it. They are already here and there are five of them. That seems a little heavy on protection in my opinion. But from what I can tell, this Mr. Lanning has become a little paranoid after Florida. I wonder where they are doing their research, because I would hate to walk in on them the first day and lose any chance of surprise.

Do you know what Farmer looks like?" he asked while rubbing his chin in a thoughtful way.

"I may have a picture of him in my file," Mercedes answered as she opened and thumbed through her folder. Sure enough, Dr. Weston had included a copy of the mug shot that was taken of James Farmer when the sheriff arrested him in Florida. She also looked over the notes that had been added to the picture. "He is strictly security, not a researcher. We may not find him at the research site since it looks like he is probably in charge."

"That will make it a little more difficult to identify them if we see them," Desmond thought out loud. "But if several of them are bodyguards, then I should be able to pick them out of a crowd. Our problem will be that the same will be true of me."

"A disguise would help. I have an extra pair of reading glasses that we could put on you or hang around your neck. Do you have any vacation type of shirts?" Mercedes asked. "You know the ones that are light and tropical looking."

"We were supposed to blend in, so yes."

"Great, go put on shorts and a shirt, and we will make you look like the crazy tourist. If you stand out too much, they may disregard you as on vacation or something," she instructed.

Digging through his bag, Desmond pulled out a bright green Hawaiian shirt with white flowers, a pair of shorts, flip-flops, and even a baseball hat.

Laughing, she said, "I don't know if I can go anywhere with you now, you look too much like a tourist." Flinging the hat across the room at her, she ducked.

"What was in your e-mail?" she inquired.

"Mr. Swartz thinks it is a good idea to try and contact Farmer and said he would try and set it up through the boys. That way we can know more of where they are."

"If Mr. Swartz sets up a meet today, tell them to look for that shirt," she laughed again.

Desmond knew he was in for an interesting trip and that he would have to go to the store for more clothes if his wardrobe was going to stir up this much ridicule.

After he and Mercedes responded to their e-mails, they picked up their backpacks and headed out the door. Walking actually sounded nice to Mercedes, so she and Desmond went out hand in hand to give the appearance of affection. As they walked along, they looked at the shops and even found a place to have lunch when that time came. They arrived at the museum in less than ten minutes, and Mercedes went to the director's office to present her credentials. She was hoping to be able to gain access to materials that were not openly on display.

The museum director, Ignacio Montalvo came out of his office. "Greetings, Ms. Benavides. Won't you come into my office please."

"Thank you. This is my boyfriend, Desmond White, who is helping me with my research," she said.

Ignacio Montalvo's office was small and stuffed with all kinds of artifacts, books, and what looked like hundreds of stacks of papers that he had not filed yet.

There was a Dominican flag, with its red and blue squares divided by a white cross and crest in the center, hanging in the corner along with a Spanish flag from the 1500s hanging in the other. Even a painting of Columbus hung from the wall adorning another area where there were no bookshelves.

"How may we help you, Ms. Benavides?" the director asked.

"I am doing my PhD work on Spanish conquistadors and have been researching Pedro Alonso Niño. My previous research indicated that he frequented Santo Domingo, so I thought I might spend some time seeing what I can find."

"We do have several works on display that cite Pedro Alonso Niño. I will make certain my staff makes them available to you. There may be other references in our collection that are not on display. I will have the person in charge of that area make a search for you if you would like," he offered.

"That would be wonderful. Do you by chance have a study carrel that I might be able to use so I am not interrupting your museum guests?" she inquired.

"That can be arranged. The only thing I ask is that in your research that you mention the museum and its collection and that you abide by our normal working hours. We will be happy to help you in any way, but I try to make certain my staff is not kept longer than they have to be."

"That is most kind of you and I will make certain that your staff will receive our utmost courtesy in return," she graciously answered.

The director led Mercedes and Desmond back out into the museum area and instructed his staff on their agreement. Immediately, a young woman led them to a small desk out of the way and informed Mercedes that this area was available as long as needed. She then led Mercedes and Desmond through the museum noting pieces that mentioned Niño. The curator gave Mercedes permission to pull each piece off display and look through it as long as she wore a pair of white cotton gloves to protect the artifacts. Mercedes was pleased to have gained the respect of the museum staff; and, from that point on, they were eager to help in any way possible.

The first few pieces were just mentions of Pedro Alonso Niño in city papers. There were references to him and his crew staying for short periods of time in Santo Domingo. There was no reference to his conquests or his treasures in any of the documents that Mercedes read that morning. But she knew that research was that way: search until you find that one clue that opens the door to more clues.

Mercedes and Desmond broke for lunch and walked to the restaurant they had spotted earlier. The small place had eight wooden tables and chairs decorated in the colorful Caribbean style. They both ordered *pollo guisado*, a stewed chicken dish with tomatoes, peppers, olives, and cilantro served with rice and *tostones* (fried plantains), a staple on the island. Mercedes and Desmond chatted as they enjoyed their chicken and the atmosphere of the quaint café.

After lunch, they searched through more volumes at the museum on the history of Santo Domingo, learning some interesting tidbits of information about Hispaniola, the governors, and even Christopher Columbus, but nothing that helped them find where Pedro Alonso Niño had discovered his treasure. At the end of the afternoon, they returned to the hotel and asked the concierge at the desk for recommendations for dinner and went out and enjoyed the beautiful sunset as they ate.

The boys back in Dallas were fit to be tied because they were not in Santo Domingo. They were the ones who found *El Dorado* after all and they felt left out. Saturday, Dalton, Juan, and Molly, who now seemed to be a permanent group member, were at Fuzzy's Tacos eating lunch when the research topic came up for the hundredth time.

"I know that you guys want to be there, but what can you do?" Molly asked. "You know the university and your parents said no to you going."

"I never thought about what we can do here to help them, I was always focused on going," replied Juan. "But what can we do here? We don't have any good information on Pedro Alonso Niño in Texas. That's the reason Lanning's team and Mercedes and Desmond went to Santo Domingo—to see if they could find exactly where he got the treasure."

"Didn't the treasure come from the mainland? If they were Mayan treasures, doesn't that limit it to where they could have found the gold?" asked Molly.

"The Mayans were mostly in the Mexico, Guatemala, and Belize, so if we focused on possible sites we might be able to narrow down the search," Dalton said with an excited tone. "We can go to the library at SMU and look from this end. They did give us passes and privileges, so why don't we go check it out."

Juan called his mother and asked if she could take them to the library, which she gladly did. Having privileges meant that the boys could go into any part of the library they desired and could request any of the material, even if it was labeled restricted. The library had been so pleased to have some of the relics from *El Dorado* that they gave Dalton and Juan the privileges as a thank you, never thinking that they would use them to continue the search. The three of them were stopped twice by library employees, thinking they were kids just messing around. Each time when they presented their passes, the library employee stood in shock for a moment. Then they proceeded to not only let them go where they wanted, but helped them find what they were looking for.

"Exactly how did you come up with these library passes?" an SMU student smugly asked, who was also a library employee.

The boys smiled and walked him over to a display cabinet that held some of the relics from *El Dorado.* There in the midst of the gold was the story along with their pictures. The employee again stood speechless. "Don't worry, everyone does that," laughed Juan.

The Central American history section of the library was where they were headed. Both immediately started searching for Mayan cities, Juan on the computer and Dalton in books. Molly stood there dumbfounded and at a loss on what to do. She had not spent the time that Juan and Dalton had researching and like most sophomores this kind of research was new to her. "Sit over here by me. I have pulled several books; you go through this one making notes on cities and locations, and I will do the same from my book. When you find a Mayan, city tell me the name and if I don't already have it on my list, you can add to it. You are going to be the expert on your cities and me on mine. Anything Juan finds we will also add to our list," said Dalton.

Quickly, Molly sat down and starting reading through her book. Dalton taught her how to skim a book like his father had taught both him and Juan just this past summer. She would look over the table of contents and then look for names. Once she found something, she read the material around it to determine if it was a Mayan city. It took her a while to get into the swing of it, but before long she was easily moving through the books stacked between her and Dalton. Frequently, they would discuss what they had found and add it to the list. It seemed almost archaic to be writing all of this down on paper, but they had not brought their computers and there was only one on the large table they were working on. It didn't seem like they had been in the library that long when a chime and an announcement was made that the library was closing.

Dalton, Juan, and Molly had been working for four hours, and it had only felt like an hour at most. The three of them had been so busy and excited about the work that they had not even stopped to go to the rest room or check their phones. Dalton called his mom to pick them up.

"That was more fun that I thought it would be. I have always hated to go to the library and research," said Molly. "I just get on the Internet and Google it, but this seemed completely different."

The boys laughed. "We felt the same way about research ourselves until this past summer, then we became excited about discovering the information we needed and found ourselves hunting for treasure not just in the swamp, but in the library as we dug in trying to look for facts and information that would help us," said Dalton. Then he added with an encouraging smile, "By the way, you did a great job."

"I had a good teacher," said Molly.

"Stop that! Now you are making me sick," cried Juan. They all began to laugh. "The library is open tomorrow afternoon, so everyone go home and we will enter what we have found on a shared document tonight. I will send you the one that I create. Dalton, add anything you found to it so tomorrow we can work on what we have not found."

After Dalton's mother drove Juan and Molly home, Juan created a document with his information and passed it to Dalton and Molly. Each read the shared information, and in no time the three teenagers had identified twenty sites, labeling each one as a city, a temple, or other sacred place. Because everyone was still excited about the work, each worked from home on the internet adding information to their sites and listing others to look up more thoroughly. The next day proved even more productive as they discovered another twenty sites to add to their list. By the end of the day, they had forty places to consider and all of this done by three teenagers.

Back in Santo Domingo, it was research as usual for Mercedes and Desmond. Both of them spent the day pouring over history books, documents, ship's manifests, but no real clues leading them toward Pedro Alonso Niño. Every once in a while, they would find something and spend the day tracking down more details, but they always led to a dead end. Mercedes was not discouraged knowing that the information was sitting out there for someone to discover and that anything worth looking for required time. Desmond, was much more anxious than that. He was use to putting a plan together and then executing it, and for the moment he did not see any results from their work. He was also becoming more concerned about Mr. Lanning's team, since they had now been on the island for five days and not spotted them yet. At least, he did not believe he had seen them. He knew that Mercedes was in charge of the work so he dutifully helped her all the while keeping his eyes and ears open for anything that looked suspicious.

The boys had contacted Farmer again and were trying to set up a time for him to meet Mercedes and Desmond. Farmer knew he needed to be careful because he did not want his cover blown as the one who was helping the other side. He finally worked out a place to meet, a bar in the old section of the city where locals went to socialize and watch soccer matches. He decided it would be best if he, Desmond, and Mercedes all made it a habit of going there but not meeting. If anyone else from Mr. Lanning's team followed Farmer, then his actions would not be out of the ordinary. If the three of them were frequently seen in the same place but not speaking, it would help their cover of finally having a drink together. The boys forwarded the information along to Desmond and Mercedes.

The next time Mercedes and Desmond returned to the museum, the director stopped Mercedes. "One of my assistants had an idea and found Pedro Alonso Niño registered as a Spanish agent for the Crown. Given this designation, the assistant looked into the government archives and found multiple references. We have placed that material at your workstation. I hope it helps," he added as he politely gestured in that direction.

"It certainly, does help!" said Mercedes. "I did not expect your staff to go to any trouble to help me, though you have definitely gone out of your way. Thank you."

Mercedes and Desmond headed to the desk and found several large old journals. She was ecstatic to have some new material to look over and hopeful to find some good leads to Pedro Alonso Niño, instead of just a few simple references. As she sat down at the desk, Desmond pulled up another chair and began to go through the stack with her. Even though they came from different backgrounds, they both were pursuing the research with equal passion. After a while, it seemed that they were working as one, looking through the journals and discussing the material that they found. When Desmond thought something may be worth noting, he would bring it to Mercedes's attention since she was the true expert and keep a record on each worthwhile find. By the end of the day, they had come across several statements by the governor that Niño had been supplying the Spanish Crown with objects of worth that were being stored in a warehouse within the citadel. It seems that each time Niño arrived in Santo Domingo, the soldiers would go out to his ship and escort his cargo back to the citadel to be locked up and guarded. Without mentioning the cargo, Mercedes knew that this was the treasure that the boys had found from *El Dorado*.

"Have you come across anything that tells you where the citadel was then?" Mercedes asked Desmond.

"No, but I did run across some maps of the city during the early 1500s that would probably help," he said. He went to the cartography desk that had several shallow drawers. Each drawer, labeled with dates and titles, contained maps carefully enclosed in protective sheets. A simple title, date, and description of origin identified each sheet. After carefully lifting each sheet, Desmond found a map of the city dated 1505. Then he began to search for the citadel beginning at the docks. He knew that they would have to be close since it was believed that the biggest threat to the city would come from the water. Within a few minutes, he found the word *ciudadela* (citadel) on the map and then located the Museo de las Casas Reales or as it was known in that time the governor's office and the royal court. Surprisingly, they were only a few blocks from the sight. He pulled out his phone and took a picture of the map, specifically the citadel and then placed it back in the drawer.

"I found the citadel on the map and it's actually nearby," Desmond informed Mercedes. "Maybe we can find a restaurant close to the place marked on the map tonight and at least see if there's anything worth visiting in the daylight."

"Dinner does sound good," said Mercedes. "And my eyes are tired from reading all of these documents. Let's call it a day and head back to the hotel, so we can clean up and inquire about someplace in that area to dine." With that, Mercedes closed up the journals, returning those she had finished with and asking the director to set the others aside for her to look over tomorrow, which he was delighted to do.

"Do you think we should contact Farmer?" she asked.

"I don't think we have enough to really share, but it would be nice to see if he has anything that would help us along. Why don't we stop by that bar and have a drink on the way back to the hotel and see if he is there and wants to make contact," Desmond suggested.

Agreeing, Desmond and Mercedes started walking the few blocks back to the hotel. They veered off their normal route to pass by the bar Farmer had recommended, which turned out to be an upbeat place with orange, yellow and red painted walls, a long wooden bar that looked like it was hundreds of years old, and all kinds of things hanging from the ceiling. Desmond couldn't figure out what the theme was because there were flags, banners, piñatas, and colored lights. The one thing that was obvious was that it attracted people who wanted to relax after a long day and visit with friends. There were mostly locals, but there were also others who were obviously foreigners. In the corner was a large TV with a soccer game blaring. Desmond found it welcoming and so he escorted Mercedes to a table that was on the patio and ordered drinks from the young waitress.

"This looks like a fun place to hang out," quipped Mercedes with a broad smile on her face. "It seems like a cross between a themed Mexican restaurant and a dive bar where only drunks hang out."

"Yea, my kind of place," chuckled Desmond.

"Do you see anyone who fits Farmer's description?" Mercedes asked.

"No, his description says he is just over six feet tall," answered Desmond. "And from the picture you showed me, he's a little overweight but not fat with sandy-colored hair. He will probably be with some of the muscle on his team and their researcher. I should be able to pick out the muscle because ex-military enforcers have a certain look."

"What about you? Aren't you an ex-military enforcer? Won't they spot you?" she joked.

"Yes, they will spot me, but I have a plan," and he reached over and pulled her chair closer to his. "They will look like they are working, I will look like I am enjoying the company of a beautiful woman," he said as he smiled at her.

"I'm your disguise," she joked, giving him a playful punch, then smiling at him with a twinkle in her eyes. "We are technically off duty," she said as she reached for the drink the waitress had just set down and lifted it in a salute. *This could be a fun evening*, she thought to herself.

They laughed and chatted while drinking, but all the while scanning the room to see if Farmer was there. They were just about finished when a mountain of a man walked through the door followed by two other large but fierce-looking guys. Desmond recognized their kind in a moment. They carried themselves as if they dared anyone to confront them and a little disappointed no one would. As they slid up to the bar, they looked his direction, but he had already leaned over to Mercedes and kissed her. A little shocked at first but not upset, she kissed him back. He slid his head down near her ear.

"The three that just came in are our guys. Farmer doesn't seem to be with them, but I would bet my life on it. They are standing at the bar just a little off to your right. Get a good look at them," he whispered.

With both a feel of regret and relief, she realized that the kiss was part of the disguise, but she laughed and blushed anyway. *It had been exhilarating*, she thought. She continued to talk as he looked at her all the while trying to keep sight of them out of the corner of his eye. She pulled out her phone and pulled away from him and started posing and taking selfies. She showed it to him and they both laughed. She took another from another direction and showed it to him again. He realized what she was about to do.

"Yes, you are beautiful, but you don't want me in your pictures?" he joked loud enough for people around them to hear.

"Sure, I do," she replied as she leaned to her left, lifting her hand up and out to get a good shot of the two of them. Just as they started to pose, she touched the button that went from selfie to picture mode and snapped the shot, catching all three men in her picture. "You, goofus, you closed your eyes," and she repeated the shot, but this time took the selfie of the two of them. "Now that looks better. I will have to post that on Instagram for all our envious friends," she laughed.

He was surprised at how quickly she came up with a plan and executed it and then even covered the picture with another selfie in case someone saw what she had done. It had crossed his mind to take a picture, but he knew that he would be noticed. However, a woman taking a selfie in a bar was common, and Mercedes had taken advantage of it. They continued to laugh, and he ordered another drink.

"Let's stay for one more drink then go to dinner," he suggested, hoping to see if Farmer would arrive. He held up two fingers and the waitress who was two tables over nodded her head and brought over two refills.

As Mercedes and Desmond continued their conversation and were about three fourths of the way through their second drink, a man and a woman walked into the bar and moved across the room to join the other three. Desmond recognized James Farmer immediately from the photo. The woman was beautiful enough to attract attention, but she didn't turn her head to notice the attention she was getting. It was obvious she was accustomed to this reaction, maybe even expected it. Even Mercedes noticed her and watched her walk in. Desmond had to bump her to stop her from looking.

"I know her," stammered Mercedes.

With a look of shock and surprise on his face, he turned to her and asked, "How do you know her?"

"That is Dr. Jacqueline Montavilla. She is a well-known archaeologist in specializing in the Aztec people.

She has written several books about the subject," Mercedes answered.

Still with a panic look on his face, "Does she know you?"

"No, we've never met. I heard her speak once at a conference, but there were more than a hundred people there so she would not recognize me. I have always wanted to meet her."

"Good, but now is not the time. I am sure before all of this is over, you will get your chance." He leaned over and gave her a hug, whispering in her ear, "It's time for us to go." With that, he left money of the table, helped her to her feet, and slipped out into the street never looking back.

He reached down and took her hand as if they were lovers and walked down the street just as the sun was setting. She started to ask questions about the encounter, but he stopped her each time, wanting to wait until they were alone. They even took a longer way back to the hotel that allowed him to see if anyone was following them just in case, which they were not. When they stepped into the suite and closed the door, Mercedes nearly burst.

"Okay, why did we leave? I thought you wanted to contact him?"

"We did contact him. While you were busy looking at the woman, he was scanning the room and caught sight of me. He gave a slight nod and then looked away. He now knows who we are and that we can be found at the bar. So, we will have to wait until he feels it is safe to contact us. That just became our new watering hole," he added.

A little perplexed, but knowing that he was right, Mercedes agreed, then headed off to change and freshen up for dinner. Desmond, likewise, did the same, but as soon as he was finished, he got on his computer to check his e-mails and contact Mr. Swartz and the boys. He thought if the boys knew they might be able to pass information to Farmer. Just as he was finishing, he looked up and saw Mercedes walk out in a short red dress with high black heels on. She walked into the room just as captivating as Dr. Jacqueline Montavilla had into the bar.

She walked over smiling. "Close your mouth, it's not attractive," she said, but secretly enjoying his reaction. "I am hungry."

Without a word, he got up and followed her to the door, down the elevator, stopping only to talk to the concierge about restaurants in the area by the old citadel. Having found one, they ordered a taxi and rode in silence all the way.

"Are you not going to say anything to me?" she asked.

"I am sorry, you caught me by surprise and have left me speechless."

"You are forgiven," she said with a smile as he helped her out of the taxi and across the sidewalk to the restaurant.

They sat at the table enjoying dinner and talking about what they had discovered that day in the museum. They talked about their next step in finding more about Pedro Alonso Niño, which included a stroll around the area. After a wonderful seafood dinner, they stepped out into the cool Caribbean breeze and began to walk in the direction of the citadel.

They had not gotten too far down the street when a man stepped out of a dark doorway in front of them. With the light behind him, the man turned and faced them holding something in his hand. "Give me your purse and your wallet," he screeched, lifting his hand to show he had a knife. Frozen in fear, Mercedes could not even get out a scream, but Desmond was immediately moving. With lightning speed, he reached across the robber and hit the knife hand with such power that he almost broke it. Grabbing the wrist with his other hand to disarm the robber, Desmond slid his right hand up the arm with such force so that it collided with the man's neck, causing the man to go limp. Before he could fall to the ground, Desmond twisted the armed hand until the blade was facing up and quickly stepped closer to kick out the back of the robber's right kneecap. As he slid to the ground, Desmond retrieved the knife and struck the man's head, knocking him out.

Standing there shocked and amazed at how quickly and how brutally he had disarmed the robber, Mercedes choked out, "Is he dead?"

"No, he is unconscious. When he does wake up, he will have a horrible neck and head ache and a dislocated arm and knee, but he will survive." Then Desmond took the knife and placed it blade down into the palm of the man's hand slicing it open so that he would have a scar to remind him never to pull a knife on a stranger again. He then reached out his hand to Mercedes and gently taking it in his own, they both stepped over the man and proceeded down the street. At the next streetlight, he looked at Mercedes and said, "Close your mouth, it's not attractive," and then laughed.

Shocked back to reality, she looked at him then chuckled when she heard her words from his mouth. "They told me you were good, but I've never seen anyone move that fast and without a single hesitation. You've obviously done that before."

"Yes, on a couple of times. SEALs are trained in hand-to-hand combat in life-or-death situations, it is just one of the things that make us so lethal," he said proudly. "Sorry if it caught you by surprise. I couldn't let a man with a knife spoil this beautiful evening," he said shyly.

Smiling, she held his hand a little tighter and walked on with him until they reached the citadel around the corner.

It was a series of old buildings with some shops on the lower level. One looked like an antiques store, and several others looked like dress or clothing shops. The one building at the very center of the complex featured a sign that marked the spot as the site of the original citadel and it included a map. It would have been the ideal place to store the treasures. A visitors' center for the area occupied the lower floor; both Desmond and Mercedes agreed they needed to return in the light of day. After walking around the buildings, they found a cab driver sitting on the side of the road smoking a cigarette and hired him to take them back to the hotel.

Arriving back in the suite, they both retired to bed, each thinking about the events of the day and wondering how the rest of the trip would turn out.

Chapter 6

The Meet

At the museum the next morning, Mercedes and Desmond immediately went back to the journals they had not finished the previous day. Mercedes picked up a new one from the stack and began to skim through it looking for any mention of Niño or the treasure. An hour into her search, she came across a reference to the treasure entered by one of the governor's agents. He described a load of gold and jewels collected from what was described as a group of Mayans in a city, brought in by Pedro Alonso Niño. All of the treasure was logged into the citadel to be guarded and then shipped to Spain.

"I saw a little restaurant near the citadel last night. I think that we are going to have lunch there today," Mercedes said while tapping on a log with her pointer finger.

"Are you already hungry?"

"I think we're both hungry," she replied shifting her eyes to her tapping finger.

Seeing her agitation, but not getting the meaning, he leaned over slightly to get a view of the book. He quickly read the reference she pointed to describing some of the treasure that had been found on *El Dorado* in a log mentioning the citadel.

"My breakfast didn't last so let's go eat," he said, beginning to stand.

In one swift motion, Mercedes lifted her phone, took a picture of the page, and then slid it into her purse. With Desmond's body blocking anyone's view, she had captured a clear picture, then scooped up the journals and shuffled them to make certain that the reference was hidden in the midst of her other papers. For security, she returned them to the director as they walked out of the museum.

"It is a beautiful day to walk," Desmond suggested as he took her arm in his and guided her out to the sidewalk and then toward the direction of the citadel. As he and Mercedes got a little farther from the museum and around a corner, he made a motion to stop. He quickly checked to make certain no one was following them. After seeing the people with Farmer, he had become more wary of being followed. And now that he felt they had a lead, he thought it best to take precautions. He scanned the street for a moment and made sure no one was behind them before they started walking again.

The restaurant was about ten blocks from the museum, so they meandered along through the streets looking at shops in the old buildings. They laughed as they looked into a window of an art studio. Front and center there was a bright painting of a dog dressed as a pirate standing on a ship. "Is he standing on the poop deck?" Mercedes chuckled.

Snorting and shaking his head, Desmond could not keep a straight face and began to laugh at her joke. "I guess any deck a dog stands on could easily turn into a poop deck," he snickered.

They walked on until they came to a sidewalk café that served Italian food. It was the one that Mercedes had seen the night before, so they chose a table that looked down the street and directly at the center building of the citadel. After the waiter took their order and left the table, Desmond nodded toward the building.

"Okay, I saw the reference, but was there something else I missed? We knew the treasure had been stored there so why the urgency to look now?"

Mercedes pulled out her phone and opened the picture back up. The whole entry in the log could now be seen and not only did it mention the treasure and Niño but spoke of a registry in the treasure storehouse.

With a puzzled look on his face, Desmond asked, "Do you think you are going to find the registry still there after five hundred years?"

"While we were looking at the place last night, there was a sign that said museum. I hope there are still records being kept that were not destroyed or moved someplace else. Our job is to chase the clues, and this is one I think we should chase," added Mercedes.

She was right. They were to chase the clues and this one was different from the rest, thought Desmond. Most importantly, she was in charge of the research, and I am in charge of keeping her safe. Who am I to question a beautiful smart woman? Most of all one I am enjoying being around. "You are the boss," Desmond replied with a smile on his face, only to have it playfully returned by her deep brown eyes and cotton white teeth.

After lunch, Mercedes and Desmond continued their walk. He pulled out his phone and saw that he had an e-mail from the boys. He touched her arm and directed her toward a shop, which would be a good cover for him to check to see what the teenagers had sent. When she noticed an e-mail on his phone, she realized immediately what he wanted. The more time she spent with him, the more she felt like she knew what he was thinking, so she turned into a dress shop on the street and went in.

She started going through the clothes rack like women do when they are cruising for that perfect outfit. It seemed like she was touching every hanger, pulling dresses off of the rack and holding them up. Occasionally, she would walk over to a mirror to see herself standing behind the dress. She did enjoy shopping, but her mind was really on Desmond, who had like most men found a chair and was sitting playing with his phone. It seemed casual enough to anyone else, but she was dying to know what had made him want to stop now instead of returning to the hotel and checking it then. She continued going through the racks, periodically taking a dress over for him to see. Finally, it looked like he was finished so she picked up a strapless cotton dress with macaws in blue and red on it and carried it over for him to approve. He smiled and nodded, so she went and tried it on in the dressing room. When she came out, he smiled at her like a Cheshire cat with every tooth showing and an almost surprised look on his face. She had found the perfect dress for her, and now he was going to get to enjoy watching her wear it.

"So, you like it?"

"Yes, it's perfect on you. Why don't you wear that tonight?" He reached out to give her a hug, but also placed his phone in her hand. "Take your time, and I will pay for the dress," he said as he removed the tag and carried it to the counter to pay.

Mercedes went back to the dressing room and quickly looked at the e-mail. The boys said that Farmer had an urgent message he needed to get to them. He wanted them to go to the bar and wait. Farmer said he would leave a message attached to the back of the trash can in the restroom for Desmond to pick up.

"Can you bring me a bag to carry my clothes?" Mercedes asked, calling from behind the dressing room door.

"Sure," he replied collecting one from the cashier. He walked across the store and reached over the top of the partial door for her to grab. "Did you get it?" he asked referring to the e-mail, but leaning toward the bag.

"Yes, I think that will do. Hey, I'm thirsty. Why don't we stop off at that bar again tonight on the way back to the hotel?"

"I was thinking the same thing," replied Desmond. "I could use a cold beverage."

They passed by the citadel and found its museum closed but noted the time it would be open. They then walked back to the Museo de las Casas Reales and spent a couple of more hours researching before leaving.

Following their previous plan, they made their way to the bar. Farmer and the others were already there at a table drinking and talking loudly.

Mercedes picked a table on the patio area away from Farmer and his crew, one in which they had an easy exit from the building if need be. Desmond noticed her choice immediately and happily sat down, waiting for their server. Once they had placed their orders, he asked the waitress where the restroom was and headed that direction. He cast a quick glance at Farmer who also caught his eye in passing.

Whatever he was retrieving must be something important, so Desmond thought he needed to play along with the scheme Farmer had cooked up. He used the restroom. After he washed his hands, he grabbed a paper towel to dry them off and threw the paper towel at the trash can, purposely missing. Walking over, he bent down to pick up the towel and at the same time slipped his hand behind wastebasket and snatched the note. No one was in the restroom, so he slipped into a stall to read its contents.

"Dr. Montavilla has something that seems important, but we cannot tie it to anything yet. It appears that Niño brought an Indian back with him on one of his trips. The Indian's name is not mentioned, but it does say that he was here for a while. See what you can find before she finds any more information. This could be the clue to the source of the treasure. When you come out, bump into me. I will make a big show and hit you. Take a dive and then cower away. I want them to see you as weak in case we run into you again."

Take a dive! I have never lost a fight much less faked one, he thought to himself with a huff and some disgust at the idea. It did make sense because now they would be searching for the exact same clue not searching for clues at large. He walked out of the restroom and eyed Farmer away from his table, standing up at the bar. *At least he won't have to contend with the others if he acts quickly*, he said to himself.

He headed back to Mercedes but by way of the bar. As Desmond approached Farmer, he bumped into Farmer spilling his drink all over him and then waited to see what happened.

"You idiot, you spilled my drink," Farmer yelled.

"Don't worry!" yelled Desmond. "You've probably had too many of them already, old man."

With that, Farmer balled up his fist and hit Desmond in the chin. No one could see that he loosened his fist and pulled up a bit as he made the connection to his jaw. Desmond went sprawling across the floor, and Farmer was right there on top of him, quicker that he expected. *The old man is quick*, he thought, and then immediately went into his act. He shuffled backward on his butt, pushing with his legs and holding his hands up screaming. "I'm sorry, man," Desmond hollered with a slight quiver of fear in his voice. "Please don't hit me again. I was wrong. I'll buy you a new drink. I just came in to have a drink with my fiancée.

Farmer stopped. "Don't you ever underestimate an older man again, you punk kid," he bellowed, straightening up and heading back to the bar. His friends had already gotten up and were moving in to help, but Farmer waved them off. "I can handle myself," he grunted, and they slid back into their seats at the table.

Desmond picked up the chair he had knocked over while going down and took a different route back to the table. As he approached, Mercedes's eyes were wide with fear. He looked her in the eye and motioned for her to sit back down, all the while rubbing his jaw for effect. She leaned over and checked to make certain he was all right, but he lovingly brushed her hands away and picked up his beer. He quickly waved at the waitress and left money for all of their drinks, including Farmer's, on the table. He then reached out for Mercedes's right arm helping her up and ushering her out of the bar as if he were ready to run.

Mercedes didn't know what to think of all of it. She had seen how quickly he had dispatched the man with the knife a few nights ago, but today he was a wimp. There must have been something to all of that show, but she could not figure it out and knew that asking now would be useless. They walked two blocks and turned the corner with her feeling like she was about to explode. "What was all of that about? You let him hit you and then you cowered away from him?" she blurted out in one breath.

"It's all right. It was all part of Farmer's plan. The information he gave me is going to put us on the same track, and he wanted his guys to underestimate me. I know I hated being the patsy, but it was a good strategic move."

"What did he give you that was so important?" she asked, dying to know.

"I will show it to you back at the hotel," he answered, still feeling a little sting on his jaw. They continued walking in silence. When they reached their hotel, they took the elevator to their floor. Mercedes was almost in a run to reach their suite, curious about what was so important.

As soon as the door was closed behind them, Desmond handed Mercedes the note. She quickly read it and then looked up with a laugh. She had gotten to the part about throwing the fight and knowing Desmond, she knew that that was the part that he had focused on. Losing face in front of people was difficult for a Navy SEAL, but he had played his part well.

"So, what do you make of the Indian who was referenced in their research?" he asked.

"I'm not sure. I have not seen anything about it in our work. But if that is what they are focusing on, then there must be some big reason. Dr. Montavilla is good at what she does." Thinking out loud, Mercedes went on, "This could be an Indian from the tribe who possessed all the gold Niño seized. Maybe a traitor who helped him, so he had to bring him back to save him. Maybe she is thinking if she can find anything on him, she might be able to narrow down the city."

"I think you have just as sharp a mind as this Dr. Montavilla you think is so great. That and she wouldn't look half as good as you do in that dress," he shyly replied.

"Flattery will get you everywhere," she laughed while slapping him on the arm. "Let me freshen up and take me to dinner," she demanded.

Despite a relaxing time at dinner, Mercedes did not sleep well that night. She spent most of it tossing and turning about where she might find something on this Indian … and thinking of this handsome young man she was beginning to fall for. She needed to keep it professional and not let other things get in her way. This kind of search was every archaeologist's dream, and she didn't need a relationship mess it up. She finally slipped off to sleep, but Desmond seemed to control more of her dreams than did the treasure.

The next morning after breakfast, they headed out to the citadel as planned. She could not think of any reason to go anyplace else to search, and following the treasure seemed to be their best option. They walked in the morning bustle of the city and at one point he slipped his hand over to hers and she naturally held it. It seemed so natural to her. *And weren't they supposed to pretend to be engaged?* she thought. She smiled on as they walked the ten blocks to their destination.

They entered the museum portion of the citadel and approached the clerk at the counter. "I am an archaeology student doing research for my PhD and was wondering if you had any of the original records from the citadel," Mercedes inquired while showing the person her school identification card.

"Yes, most are not on display because of the condition that they are in," the clerk responded.

"We have spent the last week researching at the Museo de las Casas Reales and found several references to the citadel and decided to visit. May we have access to the logs?" I am sure the director there would vouch for us if you want to call," she implored.

"Normally no, but given your credentials, we will allow you access if you wear gloves to protect the pages."

Mercedes reached into the backpack she carried and removed several sets of cotton gloves, which made the clerk happy. Desmond and Mercedes were led into a room that appeared to have been the actual vault, and the clerk retrieved ten separate logbooks and placed them on a table. "Thank you so much. We will not be in your way and please let us know in plenty of time to return the materials so you are not late going home," Mercedes politely interjected.

As soon as the clerk left, Mercedes and Desmond divided up the logbooks and began looking for any reference to Pedro Alonso Niño, the Indian, or the treasure. It did not take long before the treasure began to appear in the logs. There were lists, much like what they had seen in the museum, but these were very specific counts and amounts as if they were the inventory to be guarded. Niño's name began to appear beside the treasure and references to his ships being unloaded and the contents guarded here in the citadel. None of the official logs seemed to provide any more information than what they already knew.

Desmond and Mercedes took a break for lunch and even offered to bring lunch back for the museum clerk, but she declined. They walked to a small café on the citadel premises and shared tacos and Cokes before returning to the work.

They were almost done with the logs when they came upon a journal from one of the soldiers who had guarded the treasure. It was in Desmond's stack so he started flipping through the writings. Most were about his family in Spain and the young lady he had met here in Santo Domingo. He wrote of meeting Christopher Columbus and even helping Pedro Alonso Niño with his ships. Nothing seemed to important until he began writing about an Indian he had met from Niño's ships. He wrote of the unusual clothing and the language that the Indian spoke and even a crazy game they played by kicking a ball. Most of all, he wrote of the place where the Indian had come from. A large city with pyramid like altars, which he described as mountains. Desmond stopped and reread it, then took out his phone and took pictures. That caught the attention of Mercedes who was up to her eyeballs in more lists of treasure.

"What did you find?" she asked moving closer to him.

With a huge grin on his face, Desmond said, "I found the clues we have been looking for!" He slid the journal over to Mercedes and she read them.

Both of their hearts were now beating at ninety miles an hour as Mercedes read through the journal. She stopped at the description of the place and reread it. She knew immediately they were going to Mexico and joined Desmond with a Cheshire cat smile.

They agreed to continue researching to see if any other clues were hidden in the journals, but most were about life there in Santo Domingo. Having exhausted all of the leads at the citadel, they packed up the materials, returned them to the clerk, and headed back to the hotel. On the way, Desmond sent the picture of the entry in the journal to the boys for them to see.

Mercedes called Dr. Weston as soon as they walked into the suite, to explain what they had found. After a long conversation about their research and their find, it was decided that they had enough information to move their research to Mexico. Getting off the phone, she informed Desmond of the decision and they both went to pack. Dr. Weston's office would schedule flights back to Dallas for the following day. After dinner, they headed to bed awaiting a new assignment and new challenge.

Chapter 7

Mexico in the Fall

Mercedes and Desmond arrived in Dallas late the following evening, and each headed back home to unpack, wash clothes, and finally sleep in their own beds. The next day was Sunday. The rest of the SMU team wanted to give them time to decompress and relax before meeting on Monday morning in Dr. Weston's office to go over their finds and to put a plan together. Both Dalton's and Juan's parents agreed to allow the boys to miss school for the day to participate in the meeting. Gathered around a conference table sat Dr. Weston, Mr. Swartz, Mercedes, Desmond, Juan, Dalton, and Dr. Miller.

Someone in the group began to kid Desmond and Mercedes as soon as they arrived. "You were in the Caribbean for more than a week and you look paler than when you left."

"Very funny, the only time we were outside was late in the afternoon and going out to dinner. I didn't even get my bathing suit wet," Mercedes complained with a mocking smile.

Everyone settled down and began to look over the things that Desmond and Mercedes had found. The team scanned the logs and journals and put them up on a screen for everyone to read. Dr. Weston and Dalton could not read the Spanish, but everyone else who could was willing to translate the words as the team members walked through each line.

Dalton handed over the research that he, Juan, and Molly had been doing about possible sites in Mexico, which they had already narrowed down to three. With this new information, it was obvious that Chichén Itzá was the site that was mentioned by the Indian. It is the only one with pyramids in multiple directions and had been previously known as a leading city and center of worship.

"We need to put together a plan before running off to Mexico. Thanksgiving break is next week," said Dr. Weston. "But I am afraid if we wait too long that Lanning's group will have found the clues and already taken anything that they find." Turning to Mercedes and Desmond, she continued, "I know it is asking a lot of you, but can you go next week over Thanksgiving and continue your research?"

Looking at each other and knowing the importance of what they were doing, Mercedes and Desmond both agreed it was best not to stop their search. "I usually have turkey for Thanksgiving, but a Mexican feast will suit me just fine," laughed Desmond.

"It is settled then," said Dr. Weston. "Take care of the things you need to at home as my staff works out all of your housing and transportation. I believe we can get some help from a friend at the National Institute of Anthropology and History, but I will need to confirm that with him. Let's meet Wednesday afternoon, and we will create an official plan then. Until Wednesday, Dalton, keep an eye on Farmer for us so we know where his team is and what they are doing. Let us know if they discover our clue," Dr. Weston said as she got up to leave the meeting.

Filing out of the room, Juan turned to Dalton and said, "We're off next week, do you think they will let us go with them?"

"Somehow, I doubt it, but call me later and let's see if we can figure a way to convince them," Dalton replied.

Later that evening, the boys talked on the phone. They discussed how they could help and what they might be able to offer the team if they went with them. Juan, thinking for a few minutes, told Dalton he would call him back because he had an idea.

Walking into the living room, Juan approached his father and said, "Dad, do you have any time off next week? I am out of school and wondered if we could do something."

Jorge Hernandez worked for a manufacturer in Dallas as one of their production managers. He had gone to work for them twelve years before as a line worker, but had been promoted to manager two years ago. "Juan, I had planned on spending time with you next week since it is Thanksgiving."

"Dad, can you take the whole week off?" Juan inquired.

With a surprised look on his face, "I hadn't planned on it, but we are retooling part of the plant over the holiday. I could check, but why?"

Juan proceeded to tell his father about the team going to Mexico and how he and Dalton wanted to go. School would be closed for the Thanksgiving break and since his father was raised not too far from Chichén Itzá, Jorge and the boys could be very helpful to the team. Juan reminded his father that he and Dalton were the ones who started all of this adventure in the first place and they had felt left out in Santo Domingo. On top of all that, the boys could spend time with Juan's grandparents, whom they did not get to see as often. Juan begged and pleaded with his father hoping he would approve.

After Jorge made a short phone call to the plant manager and then one to his parents, he told Juan. "My boss said I could have the time off and wished us good hunting, and your grandparents have invited all of us to stay with them, so call Dalton back." Juan jumped out of the chair and hugged his father and then ran off to his room to make the call.

Dalton was shocked at Juan's scheme. It had not crossed his mind, but it was logical and added more validity for them going to Mexico with Mercedes and Desmond. Even Dr. Miller was impressed and agreed to let them go if the university approved.

During lunch the next day, Dalton called Mercedes and pitched the idea. He figured if he could convince her and Desmond he would not have a problem with Dr. Weston. After laying out all of the benefits, including Jorge's familiarity with the area, Mercedes agreed. Desmond was a little more skeptical, since he was in charge of their security, but it was a public place and a local would be of help, so he, too, said yes.

Dr. Miller made an appointment with Dr. Weston and presented the idea. Given the fact that the boys were the ones who had made the original discovery and had been helping all along, he was able to make a solid case for the Jorge and the boys to join. Dr. Weston agreed having local knowledge and another adult along would be helpful, so she immediately contacted her administrative assistant to make the necessary travel arrangements. By the time their afternoon meeting was completed, all of the plans were in place for the five of them to travel to Chichén Itzá on Saturday to begin their search.

Saturday morning, the five gathered at Dallas-Fort Worth Airport to fly to Cancún, Mexico, on American Airlines Flight 1343. When they landed, Desmond rented an SUV and drove to Jorge parents' home just outside of Espita. Since it was only thirty minutes away from Chichén Itzá, the team had made arrangements to stay with Juan's grandparents and drive back and forth each day. This also gave Jorge and his son time with his parents, since they were only able to visit once a year.

They settled into a beautiful *ranchero* with horses, cows, and a cozy house that smelled of an *abuela* (grandmother), cooking for her family. All kinds of memories came back for Juan and Jorge and even for Mercedes who remembered her own grandmother's home. Dalton was mesmerized by the new experience of Mexico, because it was seeing for the first time the place that held so many fond memories for Juan. Everything seemed new and alive, with its open spaces, earthy smell, and warm friendly people. Though Dalton could not understand what was being said, he could tell by the reactions and the smiles that they were welcoming him as family.

The boys chose to sleep in the barn, a place where Juan had slept on previous visits. There were cots in a loft overlooking the tractor and tools so it felt more like staying in a treehouse. Mercedes, Desmond, and Jorge stayed in rooms in the main house close to Jorge's parents. After a wonderful meal, the boys wandered outside through the pasture with Juan telling him all of the adventures he had had here as a kid. Then each headed off to bed exhausted from the travel but exhilarated with the new adventure that awaited them the next day.

After breakfast, the five of them crawled into the vehicle for the trip down Yucatán Dzitás-Espita and Highway 79 to the sacred city and its pyramids. With Jorge driving, Mercedes talked about how they would spend the day. Her goal was to get everyone acting like tourists for the day: take the tours, see the sights, and ask as many questions as possible to create a familiarity with the site. For security reasons pointed out by Desmond, they split up into two groups, Jorge and the boys and then Mercedes and Desmond. He did not know if Farmer's group had moved on over the last two days so he wanted to be cautious for the boys' sake.

Pulling into the northwest corner of the complex, Desmond parked the SUV and they all went into the museum. Mercedes presented her credentials to the director and explained to him that they were doing research on *El Dorado*'s treasure. She conveyed to him their desire to research the connection and to prevent anyone else from absconding with any artifacts. They were all given clearance for research on the site and access to all the records and buildings. Before they could leave the museum, the director wanted a picture with Juan and Dalton, since they had become famous in archaeological circles after their find. A little embarrassed, the boys agreed after Desmond requested that the pictured not be published until the SMU team had completed their work.

Walking out of the museum, Juan, Dalton, and Jorge were able to catch an English-speaking tour of the ruins. Their first stop was El Castillo, the large pyramid in the center of the complex where they listened to the guide talk about the long history of the site. It had been established in the sixth century by the Itzá group of Mayans. They learned that the area gets its name for the two *cenotes* (sinkholes) located on and near the city. It made the perfect place to establish a thriving city and the center of Mayan life in that area of Mexico.

The boys could not resist climbing the ninety-one steps leading to the top of El Castillo where they could view the rest of the complex. Exhausted and exhilarated, they stood and looked down, wondering how a people could have made such a large and exact piece of architecture in the middle of nowhere. From the top, they could see the Skull Wall and the Great Ball Court to the northwest, the Temple of the Warriors to the southeast, and even the Nunnery to the far south. They could even see Mercedes and Desmond when they walked out of the museum. It was as if the teenage boys were flying above all of the trees and buildings looking down on the world.

They returned to the ground and continued their tour, seeing the Group of the Thousand Columns, the Temple of the Warriors, and the Market. They did detour over to the Xtoloc Cenote, which was just south of the market. This large sinkhole in the ground exposed an underground river. They were amazed at how deep it was and the fact that you could swim in its clear green water. Knowing they would be back the next day, they planned on bringing their swimsuits with them to do just that. After going down the steps for a better look, they headed back toward the Skull Wall.

Crossing the main grounds, they were astounded at the number of people who were there looking at the ruins. It had never occurred to them that people enjoyed visiting historic sites in person, rather than seeing them in books or on the Internet. Jorge, Juan, and Dalton continued their tour seeing the Jaguar Temple and the House of Eagles and then on to the Temple of the Bearded Man. Finally, the boys arrived at the thing that interested them the most, the Great Ball Court.

There were two walls on the north and south sides of the long court, which was larger than a normal soccer field. The walls stood about twenty-three feet high with large rings at different heights and had benches built into them. The benches had carvings depicting the two teams in ceremonial dress with sandals, pads on their knees, hips, and forearms. The object of the game was to put the large ball through the hoops without using their hands, much like soccer. Juan and Dalton were shocked to learn that the loser was stabbed by the winner as a sacrifice. "Do you think that is how we got the phrase *sore loser*?" laughed Dalton.

The boys imagined themselves playing with the Mayans, dressed in their ornamental costumes and kicking the ball around the court trying to score. They saw themselves as great warriors, fighting it out on this field of battle to the death and victoriously winning in the end. No one wanted to think about what happened if they lost.

Jorge, Juan, and Dalton spent the rest of the day exploring the ruins and all of the grounds, stopping only to eat the tacos that Juan's grandmother had insisted upon making and packing for them. They were surprised at the long history of the Mayans and their understanding of the stars, planets, and the solar system. The thing that impressed them the most was their ability to build all of the beautiful altars and walls with such precision using only hand tools.

The whole way back to the house, everyone talked about what they had seen and learned. Mercedes and Desmond had spent the day doing the same things that Juan, Dalton, and Jorge did, exploring the ruins. They spent some time in the museum visiting with the director when the boy and Jorge had left to explore Chichén Itzá. After Desmond and Mercedes toured the museum, they were granted access to its archives section. At the encouragement of the staff, they toured the complex with a knowledgeable historian who guided them to not only see but experience what it would have been like when the Mayans ruled the area. Mercedes and Desmond walked away with a greater appreciation of the heritage and culture of this once mighty people. Mercedes felt down deep that they were in the right place when she saw a few of the inscriptions and artistry that were also found in the treasure of *El Dorado*.

That evening, while Mercedes and Desmond were updating Dr. Weston on what they had learned, Dalton checked his computer. There was an e-mail from James Farmer that said they had found the same clues that Mercedes had discovered and that they would be heading to Mexico late Monday. That gave the SMU team only one day before Lanning's team would also be at Chichén Itzá. Dalton quickly ran to Desmond to tell him the bad news. Everyone had hoped that Lanning's people would take longer to find the clues and put it together, giving them a few days to search unencumbered. The time they had used to make plans in Dallas allowed the team in Santo Domingo to catch up. Now the SMU team needed to have a good plan in place to protect what they might find, but also to protect themselves from the mercenaries Charles Lanning had hired.

Desmond spent the evening reviewing the safety features he saw in place at the ruins while Mercedes consulted Dr. Weston and devised a plan to begin their search. She enlisted the boys to help her since they had done such a good job on *El Dorado*. She assigned them articles about recent research and discovery while she chose the more difficult task of wading through all of the archives for anything that would definitely tie the Indian from Santo Domingo to Chichén Itzá and possibly the treasure.

The next day, the team left early for the ruins, since they had already been granted access to the archives. The ride was quiet, as if they were all sitting there with their mouths taped shut. Each being deep in thought about what they needed to do when they arrived.

They went directly into the museum and were met by the director. It seems that Dr. Weston had been able to reach her friend from the National Institute of Anthropology and History during the evening, who then had placed a call to the director. The staff was even more willing to help Mercedes and the team in any way possible. He led them to a private office that would become their research center and handed each of them pass cards to allow them access to every part of the complex, including those areas that most could not go.

Desmond and Jorge were then led to the security office where they explained to the head of security what was going on. They were then taken into the room with all of the monitors for the security cameras on the property. With a map, Desmond and Jorge were able to visualize the areas that seemed to be the most difficult to monitor and then were taken out in a golf cart to see the security firsthand.

While Mercedes was off in another area of the museum collecting materials to study, the boys opened up their computers, logged into the museum's network, and began to search for articles. Remembering from their last research, they kept a record of every site they accessed on the Internet so that they could find it again if they needed more information.

Dalton came across an article about El Castillo by Elizabeth Roberts and Lauren Said-Moorehouse, describing two pyramids inside of the one they had climbed. It said that in the 1930s, a jaguar throne covered in jade was found inside El Castillo, and then in 2016, using a new type of electronic x-ray, researchers were able to locate an inner pyramid over a cenote. Dalton had never thought about what might be inside of the pyramid, he had assumed it would be solid, so this was a new thought for him. Later on, another article by Richard Gray told of a cenote growing underneath the pyramid that could at some point make it collapse. Gray said that all the cenotes are connected by an underwater river that gave life to the area.

All of this research was blowing Dalton's mind. Pyramids inside of pyramids and rivers running underground, what else could there be?

Juan was busy downloading history of Chichén Itzá when Dalton showed him the article he had just found. "Do you think they have copies of these scans here in the museum?" asked Dalton.

Amazed himself, Juan replied, "Let's find out." Then he closed his computer and got up to find one of the museum staff. He found the young lady who had helped them get all of the network log in codes and asked her about the scans and topography maps. She nodded and went into the back room to retrieve what they had and a few minutes later came out with a large folder.

Dalton and Juan spread the scans out on the table in the office they were using. At first, it was a little difficult to understand what they were looking at because it just seemed like strange bands of color underneath a faint drawing of the pyramid. In the bottom right corner, they found a legend describing the colors as different types of material and also the different depths from the outer blocks. Once they understood it, they could easily see the structure underneath El Castillo. It was fascinating to believe that there was more hidden.

Dalton pulled out another scan that looked at the ground underneath the main pyramid at Chichén Itzá and even the surrounding area. He could see very clearly the cenote under the inner pyramid and the underground river that connected the cenote north to the one south of the complex. He had read that the researchers estimated that there was only about sixteen feet of soil between the pyramid and the cavernous river that flowed as much as sixty-five feet deep below it.

"What if we could travel under the pyramid and come up underneath it in the river connecting the cenotes? Wouldn't that be cool?" Dalton questioned out loud.

"That would be cool, but I can't hold my breath that long and we don't scuba dive. It's a shame we don't have a little submarine like the one in the movie we watched in science class."

Dillon pondered that thought and asked, "Could a little submarine even get in there? Do you think it is really big enough to travel that distance?" He decided to go to the museum director to ask him about the underground river. He was surprised to learn that the river connecting the cenote had been assessed to be relatively long, but they had never done more than a dye test to see if it was connected to the other cenotes on the complex. The test consisted of dropping a biodegradable dye into the Sacred Cenote and waiting to see if the dye appeared in Xtoloc Cenote. They found they were connected and that the stream moved at a swift pace because it arrived within an hour. Unfortunately, that was the only testing that had ever done on the river.

After leaving the museum director, Dalton wanted to find Desmond to question him about the river. As a former Navy SEAL, Desmond had to be an experienced scuba diver, and he might have an idea about how to use the river to get to the inner pyramid. Dalton found Desmond and Jorge walking near the Market checking out security.

"Desmond, do you think it is possible to use the cenote to access the inner pyramid?" Dalton inquired after showing him the research he had found on the pyramid and the large cenote underneath El Castillo.

"I never thought of it, but are you thinking that we may find the evidence we need to tie all of this together inside the pyramid?" asked Desmond.

"Where else could it be? All of the artifacts here have been translated and discovered. The only thing here that still remains a mystery is the inner pyramid and its surrounding area. I know they have been trying for years to get inside, but have they ever tried access from the water?" queried Dalton.

"I don't know," said Desmond. "But I will have Mercedes check and then I will see if I can find out if there is a possibility of traveling through the cenote and underground river."

They parted ways. Desmond headed to find Mercedes and Dalton to connect with Juan. Juan had continued his search of articles but had found nothing to help them. Remembering the miniature submarine in science class, he decided to try searching for vehicles that could enter the underwater caves. Juan came upon a site on underwater drones and did some inquiries. It seems that the Trident underwater drone by OpenROV was small, lightweight, and could handle tethered extensions. He printed out the information to show it to Dalton and Desmond.

Desmond, Mercedes, and Jorge were just outside of the office they were using near the museum director's own office. When the boys arrived, they found her and Desmond discussing the underground river.

"Desmond, what if we used a drone to do the search in the cenote instead of a person? I found one here that is small and may be able to get us a view safely," Juan shared while passing around the printout he had made of the drone. "If we could get one here, we might be able to use it to see if there is access without disturbing anything else."

Desmond and Mercedes looked at the printout and began discussing the possibilities. Jorge stood in the corner with a surprised and pleased look on his face. He had not been a part of *El Dorado*'s discovery so watching Juan and Dalton interacting with these adults and the staff of the museum amazed him. When the boys spoke and made suggestions, everyone paid attention and discussed the possibilities. Jorge wondered if any other teenagers were treated with such respect by adults, especially adults with PhDs after their names. He had always been proud of his son, but this far exceeded the pride he had shown for his athletic abilities—this was about manhood.

After a thoughtful conversation, Mercedes went into the director's office and asked if they could have permission to send a drone into the cenote. She explained that not only could they try to prove their hypothesis correct, but they could also map the river and possibly get them more information on the potential of the cenote collapsing and taking the inner pyramid with it. The director was excited at the prospect, but knew that he had to get approval from the National Institute of Anthropology and History before he could say yes.

In the meantime, Desmond got on the phone to Dr. Weston to discuss the idea. He knew that the team would need money and approval to purchase a drone and would incur liability if the experiment failed. He explained to her the problem of no access to the inner pyramid and that there was a river that flowed from the cenotes beneath El Castillo. He explained that they speculated that the original pyramid was built over a cenote on purpose, meaning that there was possibly an opening inside. It was too dangerous for anyone to attempt to dive at that depth for that distance with no knowledge of whether a person could safely enter. The drone was the only solution. He gave her all of the particulars on the drone, promising to e-mail the details, and asked if they could negotiate a deal to have one delivered immediately. It seemed like a crazy idea, but Desmond thought it was worth a shot.

When he got off of the phone, Juan asked, "What did Dr. Weston say? Do you think she bought the idea?"

"I don't know. She sounded interested, but not convinced. We will know in a couple of days. The problem I see is that Farmer and his bunch will be here tomorrow. Anything we do will have to be incognito," Desmond explained with a look of despair on his face.

The boys walked away dejected. They thought they had a good idea and even the rest of the group agreed, but it looked like a lack of time would keep them from gaining entrance to the inner pyramid. People for centuries had been trying to find that out and now that they had a potential solution they would not have the time to try.

When Dalton and Juan checked their computers, they found even more depressing news. Lanning's team had arrived and were staying at the hotel near the archaeological site. They quickly alerted everyone on the SMU team and the complex's security staff. Desmond felt it was better for them to get off of the property before they were seen, so everyone packed up and headed back to Juan's grandparents' home.

It was quiet on the ride back, almost as if someone had died. Having not been at Chichén Itzá long, the five of them they had covered a lot of ground. Mercedes had looked over all of the important research on the site, Desmond and Jorge had familiarized themselves will security, and Dalton and Juan had studied El Castillo and the cenotes. It did not seem to any of them that there was anything else they could do. Their access would be severely limited with Lanning's team there. The SMU team could not risk being seen and possibly put the boys in danger. They would have to do their work remotely or at night, and neither of those options appealed to them.

Arriving back at the *ranchero*, Jorge's mother had prepared a wonderful meal and invited neighbors to come and dine with them. It seemed like a fiesta to Dalton, but to the rest, it was just a large family gathering. After everyone ate and enjoyed the evening, they all went to bed and slept restlessly. It was hard to sleep feeling that you had been defeated.

At breakfast the next morning, the SMU team discussed their plans and stayed home for safety reasons. Jorge and the boys helped Grandpa with chores that needed to be done around the *ranchero*. They nailed up some boards on a fence, fed the animals, and even got to swim in a nearby river that was on the property. It was fun being away and working and playing, but their minds were still on the pyramid.

Dalton and Juan arrived back at the house late afternoon and found Desmond with a huge smile on his face. "Guess what, boys? We need to make a run to the airport tonight."

"Really, why?" asked Dalton.

"It seems that Dr. Weston tracked down the owner of the OpenROV through some important supporters of the university who knew him. She called him at home and explained what they were doing in Mexico and asked if his drone could do the job. The owner jumped at the chance to not only help but to test his drone in the underground cave. He told her he would package one up and would send his best engineer with it to operate it. He e-mailed an hour later with all of the flight details confirming that he and the drone would be arriving tonight in Cancún," Desmond said jubilantly.

The boys cleaned up and headed to the airport with Desmond with a renewed sense of adventure. The only thing they needed now was approval from the National Institute of Anthropology and History.

Chapter 8

Cave Diving with a Drone

James Farmer's group had arrived the previous evening and settled into the hotel near the pyramids. After dropping their luggage in their respective rooms, they gathered in Dr. Jacqueline Montavilla's room to discuss their plans for research.

"We don't know exactly what we are looking for, we only know that the description by the native described some place like Chichén Itzá. Before we can begin a focused hunt, I need to spend a day looking at their archives. Take tomorrow and get to know the site by being tourists for the day," Dr. Montavilla suggested. The rest of Lanning's team thought it was a good idea to get the lay of the land. They agreed to break up into pairs and blend in with the tourists taking tours. Farmer decided he would stay with Dr. Montavilla to give her help and protection if needed. No one except him knew the existence of the SMU team. They ate dinner and headed to bed after a day of traveling.

Desmond and the rest were surprised at how small the remote-operated vehicle was. Peter Schultz, the engineer for OpenROV, collected his bags on a cart, passed through customs, and then saw Juan holding up a sign he had made with the name OpenROV on it. Three hard cases, the size of large suitcases, were stacked on Peter's pushcart along with a piece of luggage. Peter was a thin brown-haired man in his late thirties, dressed more for the office than for Mexico. He gave the appearance of intelligence with his glasses and out-of-style haircut, but with a friendly gesture he introduced himself to the group.

"My boss gave me a dossier with a description of what you were doing and it included some background on each of you," Peter said after meeting everyone in the group. "I'm not sure where he got it in such a hurry, but it included pictures."

Everyone laughed. They knew that Dr. Weston was a very thorough person and most likely had her office provide the dossier and pictures. They loaded up the luggage, piled into the truck, and headed back to the house. Jorge's parents had made room for Peter so that the SMU team could stay together.

On the drive, Dalton and Juan talked about their idea of getting into the pyramid. "I read about you guys on the plane and all about your previous discovery," said Peter. "What surprised me the most was to learn that I am here at the request of two teenage boys. This is definitely a first for me."

Desmond replied, laughing, "I know what you mean. You would see these boys on the street and just think they were kids, but we have all learned that they do their research before they present an idea. This idea surprised us at first, but when you see their research and the full plan I think you will understand why we listen to them."

The boys sat there a little embarrassed at being complimented, but were proud in the fact that they had gained the respect of the adults on the team. This whole conversation did not slip past Jorge, Juan's father. He continued to watch both Juan and Dalton as they interacted with the grown-ups, and his heart swelled with pride to see the young men they were becoming.

When Desmond, Jorge, Peter, Dalton, and Juan arrived back at the *ranchero*, they ate a wonderful meal and then sat out on the patio talking about what they had in mind. The boys began sharing their research about the cenotes in Chichén Itzá and the possibility of there being an access to the inner pyramid beneath El Castillo from the sinkhole, since the water was important to their worship. They showed Peter the results of the dye test proving the cenotes were all connected and the belief that there may be enough room for a person to travel from one cenote to another. Given all this, Peter understood why they had wanted to use a submersible drone.

"This will be a first for our drone. In the past, we have worked in open waters and even conducted inspections of wrecks, but we have never used one in a cave," Peter informed them.

"Do you have enough tether to reach the pyramid that's nearly a mile from the opening?" inquired Desmond.

"I brought enough tether to reach more than a mile so we should be good. I can set the camera to record so we can retrace the path if necessary."

Juan, thinking about the process, "Is there any way to track the drone from aboveground?"

"Since our work has been in open water and smaller spaces, we have not put any kind of tracking device on it. The best I can do is to create a map with distance, speed, and angles," Peter said with a frustrated look on his face.

Everyone was disappointed about not being able to track the drone, but knew that they could create a pretty detailed map from the video. They continued their discussion about how to launch it in the cenote and how many people they needed to help. The drone was relatively simple enough so that one person could launch and another operate it.

While Dalton showed the group the research on his computer, he noticed that there was a new e-mail from James Farmer:

We have arrived at Chichén Itzá and are staying at the hotel nearby. The plan is for the group to tour the site and get a feel for what was there while Dr. Montavilla and I do some research.

"Guys, we have a problem! The other group has arrived and will be wandering around the ruins tomorrow like we did the first day," exclaimed Dalton.

"What other group?" Peter inquired.

"Our purpose is to find any link to the original treasure and stop a man by the name of Charles Lanning from finding and taking any further treasure. He has sent another group to research and find the origins and because we stopped him last time he has employed security to make certain it doesn't happen again," Juan explained.

"Let me get this straight, we are looking for something that may not exist and trying to find it before another group does who is not friendly," Peter said with trepidation in his voice.

"Pretty much," quipped Dalton, as if it were a normal daily occurrence.

Peter sat trying to take all of this in, because he was just told they were checking out a cave, not that there was potential danger in their search. He looked around the group and saw two teenage boys, a woman, and two men. Was he ready for this?

"They have caught up with us, so we need to work smarter. I assume we can operate the drone at night since it will be in the dark in the cave?" Desmond asked.

"Sure, it works in the dark," replied Peter. "There is nothing stopping us from operating it at that time."

"We still need approval from the National Institute of Anthropology and History to use the drone, so as soon as they give us permission we will go in after-hours undetected to avoid Lanning's group. By the way, Peter, the leader of their group, James Farmer, is on our side and feeding us information," Desmond shared.

The SMU team continued to discuss their plans for the next day, knowing that going to Chichén Itzá was not an option. Peter shared how his drone worked and what they could expect to see. "It's a shame we don't have a place to try it out," Mercedes said.

"There is a pond on the property if you want to get it wet tomorrow, Peter," said Jorge. That excited everyone. How could they not be excited to see a remote-controlled submarine filming in the pond. They were going to have to wait for approval to enter the cenotes from the National Institute of Anthropology and History so they might as well play while they waited.

The next day proved to be as fun as they had expected. Watching Peter launch and then guide the drone underwater, startling fish, and even finding that old car that had been dumped in the pond fifty years ago was exciting. He even let people take turns driving the drone and filming. Not surprisingly, the boys adapted quickly to it since their lives revolved around video games and controllers.

The next day also brought the entrance of Lanning's team to the ruins. Dr Montavilla and Farmer went to the offices while Mario led Franklin and Earl to the tour area where they bought tickets. The three men, dressed casually in shorts and T-shirts, asked the guides many questions to understand the whole place. They took pictures, but not for the sake of remembering, instead to be able to lay out the whole property for their surveillance. Their tour ended before lunch. After eating, they roamed the ruins filling in with pictures and places they had not seen clearly on the tour.

For Dr. Montavilla and Farmer, it was a different story. She had presented her credentials to the lady behind the desk so as to gain access to material that was not readily available to everyone else coming to the museum area.

"Dr. Montavilla, it is so good to have you hear. I am a big fan of your work and even read your last paper on American tribal customs. How may I help you?" the docent excitedly requested.

"I am here to do some research on whether Spanish conquistadors visited this site and what they might have found," Dr. Montavilla replied.

"Oh, are you working with the group from SMU?" the docent unknowingly asked.

Shocked, Dr. Montavilla, quickly regained her composure and asked, "Are they still here? I wasn't sure if we would get a chance to see them."

"I have not seen them today, but they have been working here for a couple of days," the docent replied as the museum director walked by.

Shocked at what he had just heard, he stepped in to address the small group. After introducing himself, he led Dr. Montavilla and James Farmer back to his office and to a set of chairs that Mercedes and Desmond had sat in three days ago. "How may we serve you, Dr. Montavilla?"

"I am here to do some research on the whether the conquistadors visited this site and others in the area. Your docent was saying a team from SMU was also here researching."

Stammering with a reply, "There has been a group here from Saint Mark's University in Ohio studying sports in ancient times. They spent a lot of time talking about the ball court and how it was used in ancient worship. They left yesterday, I believe. Are you familiar with the study they are conducting?" he asked, hoping to throw them off track.

"No, I am not much into sports, so I have left that research to others," Dr. Montavilla replied, still apprehensive of the director's comment. "Mr. Farmer and I would like to set up an area to do some research and see if your staff can help us. Would that be possible?"

"We would be most delighted to help you in any way possible. If you will remain here for a few minutes, I will make the arrangements for one of my staff to personally assist you and find you an adequate place to work." The director excused himself and found one of his assistants who knew the arrangements previously made with Mercedes and the rest of the SMU team. He instructed the young man to be helpful to them, but to make certain that the two groups were on opposite sides of the facility. He also gave strict instructions to not give Dr. Montavilla any of the material that Mercedes was using and to report immediately to him if she and Farmer found anything of value.

With a complete understanding of his job, the director's assistant had a place cleared for Dr. Montavilla to work. He then stepped into the director's office to be introduced to Dr. Montavilla and James Farmer. "I have a place set aside for you to work, Dr. Montavilla, and will be personally assisting you. If you both will please follow me, I will show you to a study carrel and will see how I can help you."

With that, Dr. Montavilla and Farmer expressed their thanks to the director and followed the assistant through the door and across the museum. He placed them in a quiet area out of the way and a distance from the main archives, explaining that this area would create the best place for her to spread out and work uninterrupted by others in the museum. He offered them something to drink and a simple request form they could use to procure the documents she would need.

"Did you help with the group from Saint Mark's?" she asked him.

Having been previously briefed on the conversation, he responded, "Yes, they were just a couple of grad students who were really finding a way to travel and play while researching. Are you interested in their work? I could happily pull the material they had requested for you if that will help your study," he replied.

"No thank you, just curious about others researching in the area," Dr. Montavilla politely replied.

The assistant then left, stopping at the closest docent's desk to speak to the docent about taking care of Dr. Montavilla's requests. He quietly explained the situation to make certain that she was helped but also watched.

Dr. Montavilla went about setting up her computer and logging it into the Wi-Fi with the password provided by the director's assistant. As she did this, Farmer wandered around the area getting an idea of who and what was in the general vicinity, since he was in charge of security.

With what she had learned in Santo Domingo, Dr. Montavilla began to research possible connections to the Indian mentioned in the writings she had found. She began culling through Chichén Itzá history looking for any mention of the Spanish that would fit with the descriptions that she had already found, all the while sending Farmer to look for more sources. Meanwhile, Mario, Franklin, and Earl were wandering around the complex, learning everything they could about the site. At the end of the day, Lanning's team returned to the hotel to clean up and eat.

"Did you find anything interesting today in the records?" asked Mario after they had ordered their dinner.

"I learned a lot about the people and this place, but I have not found a connection if that is what you're asking," she replied. "How about you? Did you find anything that might help us make a connection?"

"No, but I did learn about how ruthless they were to outsiders and how they even devised a ball game that could bring death to the losers," he joked. It seemed like an unproductive day, but it was the first day and they were bound to find something. They finished their meal and returned to their rooms to settle in for the night.

Franklin always had difficulty going to sleep at the end of the day. He was not much of a reader, and Mario and Earl had already gotten upset at him for watching television while they were trying to sleep. He stepped out onto the balcony of the hotel room and looked out at the rising moon and the vastness of the stars that he never saw at home in the city because of all the lights. He marveled at how many there were and how he could see the moon casting a light for miles all around him. Leaning against the railing, he enjoyed the stillness and the quiet that he never seemed to find anywhere else.

He saw what he thought were security guards periodically moving around the ruins making certain that everything was secure. That didn't seem strange since he had seen security and even cameras spread around the site on his tour. Though after a few minutes, he noticed some light coming from the northern portion of the property. He could see a vehicle driving up on one of the access roads and then several people getting out, all with lights and some carrying cases. He watched with curiosity as the guards moved close to the cenote that he had seen during the day. Slowly, they descended down the steps, and the water glowed in the darkness that could only mean that lights had been turned on below the surface. The rest of the place remained dark except this one cenote.

Caught up in curiosity and not ready to sleep, he slipped back into his room, down the stairs, and out onto the property. He avoided the guards by keeping track of their flashlights and made his way north to the edge of the cenote. With darkness as his backdrop, he found a spot where he could watch the stairs, the dock, and the people who were now busily working on it.

Desmond and Peter had been playing all morning with the ROV in the pond while the rest of the SMU team watched with amazement. There was nothing else they could do since they knew that Lanning's team had arrived and would be at the ruins that day. Everyone enjoyed the morning without much to do except be spoiled by Grandma and play with their electronics. Just after lunch, Mercedes checked her e-mail and was happy to see one from Dr. Weston entitled Approved. She immediately opened and read it only to find that the National Institute of Anthropology and History with the museum at Chichén Itzá's endorsement had approved their plans to enter the cenote to explore with the submersible. She quickly called the museum and spoke to the director setting up a time to explore. Both felt that evening was better since they didn't need the daylight to work and that would be the best time to avoid Lanning's team. They agreed on a time and place to meet that very evening.

This was the group that Franklin had seen from his hotel room and this was the group that he was now watching. At first, he did not understand what he was seeing, but he recognized the two boys immediately from the pictures that Mr. Lanning had given them. He also recognized the large guy with them as the one that Farmer had hit in the bar in Santo Domingo. He had accidentally stumbled upon another group doing research, so he stayed where he was, watching and periodically taking pictures with his phone.

The group seemed to be standing around a large case that looked like a suitcase when they pulled out a white box with a long cable attached. He had never seen a submersible in person, but he had seen shows on the Discovery channel where robots had been placed in water to retrieve things. He watched with fascination, all the while recording as much as he could on his phone.

Peter set up the ROV, and Desmond slipped it into the cenote as everyone stood on the side and watched. As soon as the drone hit the water, Peter began to manipulate the controls as he had done in the pond. It slipped up and down in the puddle of light as it cleared the lines and then slip quietly into the darkness heading toward El Castillo. Everyone gathered around the video screen that came with the ROV to watch as Peter directed it deep into the underground river.

The submersible recorded every depth, and every distance along with whatever its camera and lights could see. Initially, it seemed muddy, but the water cleared to a light green, and the cavern, where the river flowed, was surprising large. Periodically, the ROV twisted from right to left to avoid fallen rocks or debris in the river along with stalagmites, but it continued on downstream as Desmond continued tracked the distance that it had covered. It was a beautiful site as the light flashed across fish and rock formations, narrow openings, and cathedral-like spaces. As it neared the estimated distance to the pyramid, Desmond had Peter slow the ROV and begin to manipulate it to look around more. When it pointed toward the bottom, the drone picked up a strange pattern in the sand. The team's goal was inside El Castillo, so Peter ignored the pattern. After another five minutes, he stopped the submersible and began to slowly move it in a circular motion to get a better view.

While watching the screen along with everyone else, Dalton hollered, "STOP! Did you see that?"

Everyone looked puzzled because no one else had seen anything. Peter made the ROV move backward slowly and immediately stopped it when the screen glowed a darker green. He maneuvered it closer to the darkness, which they realized was straight up. As the drone moved closer and closer, it became obvious that they were entering another tunnel and were rising closer to the surface of the water. Juan caught a glimpse of something to the right, and Peter refocused the drone's camera onto something that looked manmade. Sure enough, as ROV moved closer, Mercedes recognized it as an old ladder. The drone floated to the top only to see a huge dark chasm with the ladder leading up into it.

Mercedes started to cheer excitedly and hug the boys. It had been their idea to look under El Castillo and now they had a confirmation that there was access to the inner pyramid through the water. Everyone cheered and danced as they all realized what they had discovered. The SMU team tried several times to make the submersible take pictures of the interior but were not successful.

From their reaction and hearing their voices, Franklin concluded that they had found a way into the center of El Castillo, apparently their goal. He did not understand why, but this is where their research had led them so whatever they discovered was inside. He watched as they began to retrieve the ROV with success. As soon as he saw that they were packing up, Franklin headed quietly back to the hotel. When he arrived, he immediately woke up everyone to inform them of what he had seen and to show the video footage that he had taken on his phone.

Chapter 9

Playing Catch Up

"How did they get so far ahead of us?" demanded Dr. Montavilla, smashing her hand against the table in her room. "We are just now beginning to chase down this native, and they're already here and doing groundwork. You said they have a submarine for goodness' sakes, already exploring an entrance to El Castillo through the water. That means people will be next. We can't let them succeed! We must be the ones to find what lies inside or take possession of what they find before anyone else knows about it."

Everyone in Lanning's team began tossing around ideas such as going into the cenote themselves, stopping them from entering the water, or even kidnapping them. The one thing they did agree on was that Franklin needed to go back before the sun came up and set several wireless cameras to monitor the cenote and make certain that no one takes anything out. Franklin and Earl retrieved the cameras from their room, along with flashlights. After checking for guards moving around the cenote from their balcony, they left to do their work, returning just before sunrise.

Meanwhile the celebrations were loud and constant in the SUV as the SMU team headed back to Juan's grandparents' house. They didn't know if they would find the entrance or find it as easily as they did. Not only did the boys have a great idea about searching, but they made the right choice in how to look. Juan's father continued to be amazed at how his son had helped dream up a plan that could possibly change how archaeologists viewed the Mayans. Jorge also remembered all those years as a kid, when he visited these ruins, he never dreamed that there was more there than what he saw. As he drove to his parents' home, he was anticipating the phone call he would make to brag to his wife about their son's accomplishments.

Before the SMU team and the museum director left the cenote, they had spoken about getting approval from the National Institute of Anthropology and History for team members to physically enter the underground river through the cenote and come up inside El Castillo. Their original approval had only been to send a submersible, but now they needed to investigate the river and entrance into the inner pyramid. The director agreed to make the call. He could not promise an immediate answer, but he would push them for one all the while thinking how such a discovery about the site would further his own career.

Exhausted from all the excitement, the SMU team members each headed to bed and dreamed of the great mysteries they could solve if they were given access to the cenote. Granddad's rooster would soon be crowing, though none would hear it, they would all be fast asleep.

Meanwhile, Dr. Montavilla and her team continued to make plans to take over the find at any cost. Charles Lanning gave them the authority to proceed … no matter what it involved. He was furious to learn that the boys were in Mexico ahead of his expert team and made it clear that Dr. Montavilla had to find out what the other group was searching for and to get to it first. He was not going want to lose again to a group led by teenagers.

Dr. Montavilla went to work on her computer trying to find anything she could to help her determine what the SMU team was looking for specifically while James Farmer and his thugs gathered for a more nefarious reason. They discussed their options and saw that they were limited by not having a submersible and not having the museum director on their side. At this point, all they could do was to monitor the cenote for any more activity.

Farmer and the other three men all went back to bed. They knew that the other group would not enter the cenote during the day. Dr. Montavilla was safe working in her room, so they didn't feel the need to stay up with her.

Mario did not sleep long. He knew that he was there to do a job. And even though James Farmer was in charge, he decided to come up with a contingency plan that he could put in place with Franklin and Earl if necessary—one that would include taking over the operation and winning the favor of Charles Lanning. He sent a text to Franklin and Earl telling them to meet him in his room in an hour, but not to say anything to Farmer. They understood the meaning and trusted him, so an hour later they showed up and put together their devious plan.

The museum director got very little sleep. He was so excited about what they found and the chance to see the inner pyramid beneath El Castillo that he was on the phone as soon as he could, trying to get approval for their access through the cenote. There were all kinds of questions that he had to answer and even requests of pictures from their previous search. Fortunately, Peter sent pictures to him before going off to sleep. After ten e-mails and two hours of phone meetings, he received approval from the National Institute of Anthropology and History to enter the cenote and possibly the inner pyramid. The Mexican government officials did have one stipulation: they wanted someone from their institute to be present. They agreed to dispatch someone immediately so that they could try and stay ahead of Lanning's team. The director then went to the couch in his office and collapsed, with instructions to his staff not to be disturbed for a few hours.

When the boys, Mercedes, Desmond, and Peter woke up, they found an e-mail giving them approval. They headed into Cancún to pick up scuba-diving supplies and other necessities for them to safely enter the cenote and the inner pyramid. They not only rented scuba tanks, buoyancy compensator vests, regulators, and even wetsuits to protect them from jagged rocks, they purchased underwater lights, ropes, a compact expandable ladder, and a collapsible grappling hook. After grabbing a late lunch, they headed back to the house to pick up Mercedes who had slept in and then done some more research on the supposed age of the inner pyramid and the materials that might have been used. She had searched for anything that would give them a clue as to what they might expect to find.

When the males returned from their shopping expedition, the team discussed how they would explore the cave and pyramid. They discussed all of the safety options, so that they would be prepared if they faced a cave-in or if their tanks ran out of air. There were some questions as to air quality inside the inner pyramid and so it was decided to remain on their tanks just in case. Finally, they alerted Dr. Weston about their plan to proceed that evening into the cenote. Mercedes had previously sent an e-mail before going to bed explaining what they had found along with clips of the video stream from inside the cenote.

As the sun began to set, they loaded up the SUV and headed back to Chichén Itzá excited about what they would find.

Chapter 10

Finding More Than They Expected

As soon as the SMU team arrived at the cenote, Franklin picked them up on his cameras. Lanning's team was ready and waiting in case the SMU team showed up again. "They're here and it looks like they have brought equipment to enter the cenote!" Franklin announced as everyone quickly got up to head toward the door.

Lanning's team had everything they needed already packed in some lightweight backpacks and ready to go. They had stationed Earl in the upper-floor balcony to keep an eye on the security guards. By now, it was dark and the guards could be easily tracked by their flashlights. Once they knew where each guard was, they left the hotel and headed toward the cenote, avoiding detection. They took up station the same place where Franklin had been the night before. This time, they could not only see them at a distance, their cameras gave them details of what they were doing.

The museum director met the SMU team along with Ramón de la Guardia, a representative from the

National Institute of Anthropology and History who had driven in to oversee the project. Ramón had been chosen because he was an experienced cave diver and an experienced archaeologist. He came prepared to dive with them and had even thought to bring along a device to check the air quality inside the inner pyramid.

The submersible was once more lowered into the water, and Peter immediately headed it up the cave towing an attached line. Dalton was responsible for feeding out the line from a large spool so that the line would remain taught in the water. The idea was for the submersible to check for any changes in the cave and to set a guide rope for the divers to follow and attach extra air tanks for emergencies along the way. The submersible again made it to the hole, but this time in a preprogrammed route to minimize effort for the divers and to set the line. It once again surfaced in the cenote,

With everything set, Desmond, Mercedes, and Ramón donned their wetsuits and began checking equipment. Desmond, being a former Navy SEAL, was constantly checking not only his equipment but everyone else's, making certain everything they needed was with them. The divers and Dalton had worked out a series of tugs on the guide rope to communicate just in case of emergencies.

Just as they were making their last check before entering the pool, they heard people coming down the steps. To their surprise, five people entered the cenote, three of them carrying guns. Farmer called out, "No one move," emphasizing that they were now in control. The only weapon Desmond had was the knife strapped to his leg, unfortunately, effective only in very close quarters.

"We are not here to stop you from going into the pyramid, but to be a part of the discovery," Dr. Montavilla declared, knowing that sharing credit was not in her nature. "You have gear for three, so I will take one of your places. Since I am also a diver and archaeologist, I will be going in your place," she demanded, pointing at Mercedes. At gunpoint, Mercedes had no choice but to begin to remove her gear and allow Dr. Montavilla to don it. Knowing at this point he did not have much choice, Desmond helped Lanning's archaeologist suit up.

Earl, Franklin, and Mario spread out so that they could easily cover the rest of the group while Farmer went to Peter to monitor the submersible. With a sneer, Farmer said, "Hello, boys. Looks like we meet again, but this time there are no alligators," all the while looking Dalton and Juan squarely in the face. They stood shocked. His tone and harshness didn't seem like the man they had gotten to know a few months ago in the Florida swamp. They had found him to be a genuinely nice guy. And after receiving his e-mails, they were totally surprised. But just as Farmer began to turn away from them, he gave a slight wink. Juan caught it immediately and knew that it was an act. Quickly thinking, Juan hollered back at him, "So you haven't changed even though you lost your partner in the swamp. I hoped I would never see your face again!" He quickly lunged out at Farmer, but Dalton grabbed him before he could get very far.

An uncomfortable feeling spread through the group as they settled into their preplanned jobs. Juan picked up the collapsible ladder and took it over to Desmond. As he handed it to him, he whispered that Farmer was still on their side. He wanted Desmond to know that he was not leaving them alone with four gunmen, but that Farmer was also there to help protect them. Desmond turned and handed the ladder to Dr. Montavilla. "Mercedes was supposed to carry the ladder attached to her tanks while Ramón and I carried the extra tanks to be positioned in the cave for emergencies. If you are really sharing, then you will need to share the responsibilities of the dive."

Dr. Montavilla stopped for a moment but then allowed Desmond to attach the ladder. After which, the three of them dove into the cenote, quickly bobbing up to give a thumbs-up sign and then descending toward the cave. Locating the rope and the umbilical cord for the submersible, they began following it with their lights scanning the walls. The rope had been pre-marked so that the divers would know how far they were from both the submersible and the rest of the team on the surface.

The dive was scary for Dr. Montavilla, who had only been scuba diving in open water and who had never experienced the feeling of cave walls hindering her sight and movement. It felt like a never-ending tomb with a black abyss just outside of her light. More than once, Ramón had to calm her fears and encourage her through the narrowest of passages. Claustrophobia began to set in, which could be deadly when diving in a cave. She also became disoriented, making her question which direction was up or down, a common problem for inexperienced divers. Desmond continued leading the group with Dr. Montavilla behind him and Ramón in the rear, so that she could clearly see someone else the whole time. At one point, Desmond had to remove the ladder from her back to pass it through a narrow hole in the cave, all the while trying not to stir up the mud on the bottom of the cavern with their fins. The silt from the mud, if kicked up, would cloud the water and make it difficult to see anything or even to be able to tell which direction they were going.

Ramón and Desmond continued a slow and steady pace moving in and out of chambers and around rocks and formations. When they found the predetermined mark on the rope, they tied off their extra tanks and even attached a couple of glow sticks to help them find the tanks if their lights failed. They then continued twisting and turning their way through the dark cavern until they came to a marker that told them they were twenty-five feet from the submersible.

When the three divers turned the final corner, they saw the light glowing and even saw the submersible move up and down as if it were nodding at seeing them. Peter was moving the submersible to affirm his visual of them on his screen. Once they were close to the ROV, he made it begin to rise, leading them to the surface. They watched as it floated to the top and leveled out then they mimicked its slow ascent.

Bursting through the water, all Desmond could see was darkness. Being the first to surface, he kept his regulator in his mouth in case the air was dangerous, but removed his mask. He could only see the twelve-foot-high walls that made up the cenote and the darkness overhead. When Dr. Montavilla and Ramón emerged, all their lights began to dance around like lightning in a storm, giving glimpses of what was above.

Gathering together, the three divers pointed their lights straight up and saw for the first time the walls and top of the inner pyramid. Each almost swallowed their scuba regulator, gasping at what had not been seen for close to a thousand years. From the water, they could see the stones staggering inward until they reached the pinnacle. The base of the pyramid was out of view because they were below ground level, but what they could see was amazing. Ramón reached over and tilted the submersible upward so that the camera could catch their view, hoping to give everyone the thrill of discovery that they were experiencing.

Desmond detached the air quality device that Ramón had been carrying and lifted it as high in the air as he could to take a reading. Not being familiar with more than just collecting samples, he handed it back to Ramón who read the numbers. All the readings came back as normal, with no poisonous gases detected. Looking at Desmond, Ramón lifted his thumb upward to signal it was good, and Desmond removed his regulator and took a short breath, still holding the regulator in case it was wrong. He coughed once and then took in more air. He nodded his head to everyone else, so Dr. Montavilla and Ramón removed theirs, taking their first breaths inside the rock edifice.

The air smelled stale and tasted like dirt, but it was breathable. Desmond removed the collapsible ladder that had been reattached to Dr. Montavilla's back and began to extend it while Ramón removed the collapsible grappling hook and line that Desmond had given him to carry. As each began to assemble their items, Dr. Montavilla shined her light around the walls of the sinkhole. She located the remains of an ancient ladder hanging over the edge which the SMU team had spotted with the drone. Looking at its condition confirmed that the ladder was no longer safe, but it pointed to the best place to exit the cenote. The ancient Mayans had chosen the spot for a reason, they might as well investigate it.

"Guys, over here," she called as she began to swim toward the spot where the ladder lay in ruins. Desmond and Ramón saw it, too, and followed her. When they got there, they were surprised to see a slight ledge at the bottom of the ladder. "No wonder they chose this spot," she said.

"You're the expert here, Desmond, how do you suggest we get up there since it seems to be higher than your ladder?" Ramón queried.

"If we can lean the ladder up on the ledge, then we can use the grappling hook to easily catch hold of whatever is holding this rope from their ladder. We can secure our ladder with it and then use it to pull ourselves the rest of the way up," responded Desmond, already lifting the ladder into place.

"Let me go up, I am lighter than both of you and I use to play softball, so I know I can throw and catch," Dr. Montavilla interjected as she moved toward Ramón to take the hook and rope. At first hesitating, the men agreed that it was the best plan. Desmond was reluctant to trust her, but considering the circumstances, she couldn't go anywhere without them.

Removing all of their gear and anchoring it so that it would not float off, the two men moved to steady the ladder for the ascent. Dr. Montavilla carried the rope in her clenched teeth so that she had both hands free to hold on as she climbed. When she reached the last two rungs of the ladder, Desmond held the base while Ramón helped her get the hook up where she could swing it. Leaning backward to get a better angle and then paying out some of the line, she began to swing the hook in a circle like a cowboy with a lariat. It took her a couple of tries to even get it to fly out in the direction she wanted, but finally it did, clanging into rock but not catching. She aimed again at a spot nearer in line with the other ladder and launched it through the air. It again clanked and the rope began to fall like the previous attempts, then suddenly it stopped.

"Give the rope a gentle tug, but not so hard that you pull the hook back and have a flying piece of metal coming at your head," warned Desmond.

Dr. Montavilla gently tugged and the rope did not move. She tugged a little harder with still the same results. "Watch out below!" she called as she gave it a mighty tug, but nothing moved.

"You've it hooked," Desmond said. "Now toss down the line and let me give it a pull so that we will know whether it was secure enough for a climb." Dr. Montavilla ducked down so that she would not be hit if it came off, and Desmond gave it a tug with all his strength. It didn't move. Dr. Montavilla climbed down to allow Desmond to go up first to secure it properly, which he did using he powerful upper body strength to get him over the edge. He wasted no time going to what turned out to be a pillar and tied the rope securely to it, then he tied several loops in the rope to be used for foot and hand holds. He pitched the rope back over the edge and helped Ramón and Dr. Montavilla reach the top. All this time, Desmond had only been focused on the rope and had not taken the time to look around.

As Ramón climbed the ladder, his light immediately landed on the pillar that secured the rope. It was a tall carved piece of stone that rose to the ceiling to support the inner pyramid. Ramón had seen the design before but not at Chichén Itzá. He turned to help Dr. Montavilla get up and afterward played his light across the whole interior. Dr. Montavilla, Desmond, and Ramón all stood speechless in this huge room filled with carvings, drawings, pillars, and an area for worship.

Ramón immediately pulled out the camera he had tucked into his dry bag and began shooting pictures. He even switched the setting to panoramic so that he could record the locations of everything. He could not see, because of a pillar, what stood in one corner of the room: a statue of Yum Cimil, the god of the underworld. When Dr. Montavilla aimed her light across the sculpture, it sparkled. As a moth to the flame, she headed toward the gold creature.

"Don't touch it!" called out Ramón, who wondered if it was protected by booby traps. Dr. Montavilla stopped immediately, knowing it was better to proceed with caution. She moved close enough to take clear pictures and to describe it to Ramón as he was still photographing the whole room.

"This statue represents Yum Cimil with his skeletal structure and vacant eyes. He was considered one of the most dangerous gods of the time, because he would sneak into villages and take people. It is said that when he took them he tortured them by lighting them on fire. And just as they began to scream, he would extinguish the flames with water. When they begged for more water, he would light them again, repeating this over and over until they no longer screamed. He would do that until their souls were completely destroyed. In fact, if you look where you are standing, it appears you are standing in a circle like a fire pit where they sacrificed people to him," pointed out Ramón.

Jumping back and out of the circle, Dr. Montavilla shivered at the thought of what must have gone on in this place more than a thousand years before. She looked around and saw that every drawing and carving depicted the exact scene that Ramón had just described and she almost threw up right there.

"I read somewhere that after a sacrifice that they threw the bodies into the cenotes, is that true?" asked Desmond.

"That is what we have discovered in other places. Did you search the bottom of the cenote with the submersible?" inquired Ramón.

"We were so busy trying to find a way in we looked every direction except down. I will see if I can ask Peter to use the submersible to investigate your theory while we continue our work here." Desmond crawled back down the ladder and swam out to where it had been floating, keeping the guide rope line the three of them had used tight. He untied the line and found a place to tie it off and then moved in front of the camera and tried to communicate with Peter that he wanted him to look at the bottom of the cenote. He did this by lifting his fingers to point at his eyes, then pointing them out and around and then finally down. With the final downward point, Peter made the submersible move up and down as if it was saying yes.

But then the submersible did something strange, it twisted and pointed toward the rope he had just tied off. Desmond looked at it and then pointed toward the rope and the submersible nodded again. Wondering why, he swam over to the rope and give it a tug to signal he had the rope. Quickly, he felt multiple quick tugs, which was the signal for danger. Now feeling helpless, panic rose in him and knowing that with such a rude system of communication he could not know what danger was happening.

He hurried back to the ledge with the ladder, climbed up, and found Ramón and Dr. Montavilla discussing the statue and all of its legends. He got Ramón's attention and quietly told him what he had just learned. He did not dare involve the archaeologist from Lanning's team. He didn't want to alert her to his knowledge of something going on with the ones aboveground.

Back at the cenote landing, things had gone from uncomfortable to frightening. Franklin, Earl, and Mario had at gunpoint zip-tied Jorge's, Mercedes's, and Juan's hands behind their backs and sat them down against the wall. They allowed Peter to continue driving the submersible and Dalton to tend the line in case there was a problem. Lanning's bodyguards knew that if these two did not respond to the three people in the cave they would suspect trouble. Discovering treasure and bringing it back was the main objective, and they could not allow anything or anyone to alert the others.

Peter's and Dalton's answers had been normal and for the most part unseen by Mario, Franklin, or Earl. They tried to respond as naturally as possible but still communicate the danger that was happening outside. Peter replied affirmatively to Desmond's command and then pointed him toward the rope. He had no other way to communicate, but he knew that Dalton could. Peter gave a sideways glance to Dalton who not only saw it but understood what he had just done. He knew if the rope communications came alive he was to quickly respond without being seen. Turning his body at an angle where his right hand could not be seen on the rope, he felt a tug and he responded with their preplanned danger signal. In the process of him signaling, he acted like he slipped in the water, which covered up any appearance of communicating with them. He just hoped that the message got through and that it was understood.

Back in the cave, Ramón continued photographing the whole inside and then creating video panning over everything within his sight. Desmond worked with him using his light to help illuminate the areas, all the while discussing what they were going to do. They felt Dr. Montavilla would want to remove the statue, much like Ramón did because it was the only one of its kind.

"If we bring it out, then we have the chance of losing it to them if they get away. If we leave it saying it is too heavy without other equipment, then we have a chance of saving the piece from disappearing. I am not sure any of them dive so they have to keep us around to help Dr. Montavilla retrieve it," explained Desmond in a low hushed voice.

Ramón was not use to thinking about long-term consequences, since he mostly studied what happened in the past. Since Desmond's specialty was handling difficult situations as a Navy SEAL, he agreed. He did not look forward to diving a second time into the cave, but he also didn't want to lose this great find to a greedy man who cared little for history other than its value. This was his chance to make a great discovery, and he did not want it to end up in the wrong hands because of his own desire for fame.

As they finished taking pictures, Desmond and Ramón discussed what they might find when they surfaced in the cenote. Best case, the others were just being detained; worst case, they were all dead. Since Dalton was able to signal and Peter was still commanding the drone, they felt that everyone for now was still in one piece. Their goal would be to not do anything that would cause the others to get hurt and then assess the situation and search for a way to resolve it. Desmond warned Ramón that they would have to work together and possibly do things that would be dangerous. He told Ramón to follow his cues and do whatever he was told. Ramón had never been in the military and was not aggressive by nature, though he understood that lives now depended upon what the two of them did. He was completely dependent upon Desmond to give him directions and he made the decision to follow them without question, no matter what it was.

As Ramón and Desmond finished talking, Dr. Montavilla announced she wanted to remove the statue. On cue, Ramón began to make excuses about its size and weight and not having the appropriate equipment and protection to remove it safely. Everything he said was correct, though he knew they could have rigged a litter with the ladder to get it out. Desmond just listened with appreciation for the argument Ramón was making and thinking that he was doing exactly what was needed to be done to save them and the others. He felt relieved; he didn't want to face what lay ahead of them without someone on his side.

Desmond crawled down the ladder and into the water, donning his scuba equipment and giving three tugs on the rope, the signal that he, along with Dr. Montavilla and Ramón, were preparing to return. Dalton announced the signal to Farmer and the men and Peter stopped his search to go see if Desmond needed any help. He saw the three divers returning to the water and was pleased when Desmond mouthing to him that he understood the danger signal.

Checking everyone's equipment again, the three divers submerged and Desmond took the lead, with Dr. Montavilla then Ramón following as before. Without the attached line, the submersible followed along with them, providing light so that they did not use up all of their batteries. As the three of them neared the halfway point, they checked their air and realized that Dr.

Montavilla had used most of her air while the two guys had plenty to get back. She had been very nervous in the cave, breathing harder was expected, which was typical for less experienced divers. Ramón helped her change out her tank and they continued swimming.

Desmond purposely got way ahead of Dr. Montavilla and Ramón. When he approached the opening of the cenote, he removed his tank and swam underwater to the opposite side of the cenote to remain hidden and away from the lights and anyone's line of sight. He slowly ascended and came up against the far wall in the shadows. He watched as Dr. Montavilla and Ramón emerged and the surprise on all of their faces seeing Jorge, Mercedes, and Juan cuffed and sitting against the wall.

"Where's the other guy?" hollered Mario.

"He was with us until we stopped to change tanks. He hasn't come up yet?" Dr. Montavilla asked.

"No," Mario responded with frustration in his voice. Turning to Peter, he said, "Take that thing back down and look for him." Then turning to Franklin, he ordered, "Get the Mexican guy out of the water and zip-tie him also."

Peter saw the tank on the bottom from a distance and immediately panned away so that no one would see it. Earl was standing behind Peter to watch the screen, so Peter kept moving the sub all around while he worked his way back up the cave in his search. He had no idea where Desmond was, but he figured it was his job to keep him concealed as long as he could. Earl just stood there hoping to spot Desmond but not really knowing what he was seeing through the viewer.

Desmond quietly climbed up vines hanging on the backside of the cenote, while everyone was looking in the water. Given all the guns out and innocents in the way, he decided that he could not confront them without someone getting hurt. He made it up to the SUV and retrieved a phone from the console. Instead of calling the police, he called Mr. Swartz, head of SMU security. He remembered a conversation that the two of them had about operations they had both run, since Swartz had formerly been a U.S. Army Ranger. He recalled Mr. Swartz talking about some guys who did covert operations as independents, so knowing he needed help he made the call. Mr. Swartz answered on the second ring. Desmond described the situation, and then he queried about the covert group. Mr. Swartz agreed to give them a call. After learning what was in the inner pyramid, he thought that it was the best option. He instructed Desmond to keep Lanning's people in sight and to give updates. After their conversation ended, Desmond slipped back to a place where he could watch from a distance.

Chapter 11

Kidnapped

Lanning's people wanted to find Desmond. So, they asked Peter to use the submersible to search, even going all the way back to where the reserve tanks were stored. The three tanks were still there. But, with the battery running low, Peter turned the drone around to head it back to the entrance of the cenote.

"Why are you turning the submersible around? Keep searching for him," demanded Mario.

"I am running out of power," answered Peter. "I have just enough to get it back and retrieve it." It wasn't the complete truth. There was a little more power than that, but it gave Peter a good excuse to not search anymore. He did not want to stumble across Desmond somewhere accidently.

As the submersible floated over to Peter, Dalton was told to help bring it in. He lifted it up out of the water, and Peter disconnected the umbilical cord putting it back into the case. Dalton got out of the water while Jorge, Ramón, Mercedes, and Juan were led back up the steps. Only Peter's and Dalton's hands were free because they had to carry the equipment. Instead of returning to the SUV, the SMU team, less

125

Desmond, were marched toward the hotel and through the patio door of Dr. Montavilla's room on the ground floor. No one saw them enter since it was one thirty in the morning.

As soon as the SMU team members came into the room, Mario stuffed each mouth with a washcloth anchored with a hand towel around the head to keep it in place. Peter was told to plug in the submersible for recharging and then both he and Dalton had their hands zip-tied and then gagged like the rest. Finding a seat on the floor over by Juan, Dalton plopped himself down exhausted from carrying the equipment that far.

"Now what are we going to do with them, Mario?" Farmer inquired furiously. "You're the one who decided to make this physical so what's the plan? What are you going to do about the loose end still running around? How are you going to deal with these people in a hotel room? You didn't think this through and now you have endangered all of us."

"We'll keep them gagged and tied in the room and stand watch over them," declared Mario.

"What about the cave and the golden idol that Jacqueline was talking about? How are you going to retrieve it? I assume you don't scuba dive. Are you going to make her go and get it? From the pictures, it looks too heavy for her to carry," bantered Farmer.

"Just shut up! I have had enough of you, old man. Last time, the kids got the best of you, but I am not letting that happen again," screamed Mario. "I will have your job after all of this is done."

Everyone was watching as this argument transpired. They could see the breakdown in leadership happening right before their eyes. It was obvious that Dr. Montavilla wanted to be the one to get the glory for the find but didn't want to be a part of kidnapping. Now she was caught in the middle. She also knew that she could not get the golden idol out by herself and that going back in was almost too frightening for her. She was definitely in a quandary.

Mario set a schedule to guard the prisoners, and Earl took the first watch. They pulled the mattress off of the bed and leaned it against the wall so that it would create a sound barrier between their rooms. Farmer had the room on the other side of Dr. Montavilla so they did not need to soundproof that wall and it gave them a connecting room to meet. Before heading to Farmer's room, Dr. Montavilla led Mercedes into the bathroom.

"I am sorry. This is not what I intended, but I don't know what else to do. I promise I will do everything I can to make certain they do not hurt you," she said with tears in her eyes. Mercedes nodded. Then Dr. Montavilla led Mercedes back into the room where the rest of the SMU team were being guarded.

Desmond followed the group back to the hotel and watched at a distance. Reconnaissance was nothing new to him, so he watched and made a mental note of everything he saw. He knew exactly which patio door they went in and then watched as the light in the room next to that one came on. Obviously, it was an adjoining room. He kept an eye on the patios and watched for any other lights coming on that late at night. Twenty-five minutes after Lanning's people arrived back at the hotel, a room light lit up on the fourth floor, possibly another room of theirs. He snuck up close enough to see through the part in the curtains of the lower floor and there sitting on the floor were Jorge, Peter, Ramón, Dalton, Juan, but no Mercedes. He started to move to the next room but then saw Dr. Montavilla bring her back into the room from the bathroom. At least it looked as if they were trying to take care of them, even though he could see that the men and boys were bound and gagged.

He moved back away from the patio door and waited, hoping to see who would be guarding them and how often the shift changed. It was obvious that the larger of the guys was remaining to guard for the time being. Desmond slipped over to the other patio and could see James Farmer and Dr. Montavilla in the other room in a heated discussion. He couldn't hear what was being said. But since Farmer had been on the SMU team's side all along, Desmond hoped that Farmer was trying to figure out a way to help them.

There was a heated discussion going on between Farmer and Dr. Montavilla.

"What happened while I was in the cave?" demanded Dr. Montavilla.

"Mario and his boys, unbeknownst to me, took over," Farmer told her. "I had no choice but to go along. I am against hurting anyone, my job was to help you and provide protection, not kidnap anyone."

"I don't want to be charged with kidnapping, especially in Mexico. What can we do?" whispered Dr. Montavilla. "I want the idol and the glory, but not at the expense of rotting in a Mexican prison cell."

"For now, we need to play along because they have us outnumbered," Farmer told her. Dr. Montavilla nodded her approval and went about collecting her clothes and showering from the dive earlier in the night. Farmer went to his computer, but his only contact had been with the boys. He did not have anyone else's e-mail address. All he could do was hope that either Desmond got out and was able to get help, or he would find a time to free them himself.

At around three o'clock in the morning, Desmond's phone vibrated. Seeing that it was Mr. Swartz, he moved farther away from the hotel to quietly take the call. "I have two people in route to you now on a private jet. They have arranged for some weapons to be available from a friend they have in Cancún along with a car. When they arrive, they will contact you through this number. Their orders are to help you free the team," Swartz stated and then, waiting for a confirmation from Desmond, hung up the phone.

Chapter 12

Help on the Way

Two hours almost on the dot later, Desmond's phone vibrated. It was a simple message. "Arrived, heading your direction, will meet you at El Castillo at six thirty." Desmond responded with a thumbs-up emoji and waited. While he waited, he noticed that there was a change of guards over the captives. The one named Franklin came in to relieve Earl after four hours, which told Desmond that they were taking four-hour shifts.

At 6:20 a.m., Desmond left his spot and moved quickly to the pyramid. He didn't know who he was meeting so he wanted to be cautious. Whoever Swartz sent would probably have his picture, but he was blind to who was coming to him.

At exactly six thirty, a single figure appeared. The sun was just coming up, and he made his entrance with the rising sun to his back. This kept anyone from identifying him, but allowed him to identify anyone in front of him. Desmond stepped out of the shadows and stood at the foot of El Castillo. He knew that he presented himself as a target, but he also knew where the kidnappers were so it was a minimal risk. As he stood there, he heard someone call the name of his former unit. He relaxed, only Mr. Swartz would know that name. He responded with a hand signal that only special forces soldiers would know and the mood lightened as the figure approached.

Standing before the former Navy SEAL was a man strongly built but a couple of inches shorter than Desmond. They shook hands, and Steve Williams introduced himself to Desmond. Then another man appeared and joined up with them, introducing himself as Joe Garland. The two men were also military specialists, both Army Rangers, just as Mr. Swartz had been. Then the three of them headed toward the hotel as Desmond filled them in on the latest developments. He included his evaluation of the capabilities of the three guards and Farmer potentially being on their side. When they arrived at the hotel, Desmond pointed out the rooms that were being used, so Joe entered the hotel to do some reconnaissance on the fourth-floor room. He placed a small camera to track any movement in and out of the room Desmond had identified.

"How do you see us proceeding?" asked Steve to Desmond.

"I was thinking that if we can wait long enough for Farmer to stand guard we have a better chance of getting in and out without anyone getting hurt. A shooting war is out of the question since there are hostages spread out around the room. My suggestion is wait for them to go to breakfast or for all but the guards to be there and hit both doors and the door to the adjoining room. Take the extra room first quietly then we have them completely covered. We can move everyone to the museum security office if needed."

"Risks?" Joe queried.

"Gunfire from the guard and stray bullet to hostages, another guard stepping in unexpectedly, or the others seeing us and following," responded Desmond. Everyone agreed and decided that Joe would take the other room and would cover the other two and the retreat. Joe reached in a backpack he was carrying and removed three Berretta M9s with silencers and an extra magazine for each. They had smoke canisters and flash-bang canisters but decided that with only one person they risked disorienting the hostages and making it harder to escape. He also pulled out small crowbars to pry open the doors.

By 7:45 a.m., Mario, Franklin, and Earl along with Dr. Montavilla and Farmer had congregated in Farmer's room. Joe slipped up and set a listening device on the glass to hear the discussion. Mario had taken over and was directing everyone, including Farmer. "Farmer, you and Jacqueline remain here while we grab a quick breakfast and get some juice and rolls. Mess this up, Farmer, and I will personally shoot you," he sneered. The three left the room and Farmer went back in with the hostages.

Joe rejoined the two. "Let's go now, three gone, Farmer and Dr. Montavilla left. I will take her, you two take Farmer." Everyone nodded, and Steve moved into position while Desmond popped the door for Joe and then moved to his position. He waited thirty seconds and he hit his door at precisely the time he and Steve had agreed upon.

Joe caught Dr. Montavilla by surprise as she was coming out of the bathroom. He was able to quiet her and then pulled out zip-ties and towels and did the same to her that Lanning's thugs had done to their hostages. Seconds later, he stepped to the adjoining door and opened it just as the others came through.

Farmer was caught off guard by the surprise attack, but he did not draw a weapon or fight back. As soon as he saw Desmond, he threw up his hands in surrender. Steve and Joe moved in quickly freeing the hands of the hostages with K-bar knives that they drew from their backpacks.

"Everyone up quickly. We need to move as fast as we can to the museum security office. Jorge, you know where it is so you will be responsible for leading the group. This is Steve, he is your cover, follow his orders, and only stop if he tells you to stop," Desmond directed. Turning to Farmer, whom Joe had been covering. "I assume you did not put up a fight because you were on our side. Is that still the case?"

"Yes, but now I will be in trouble when they come back, because Mario is crazy. Shoot me in a non-vital place and bruise me up. I know it sounds crazy, but if they think I am still on your side I might be able to communicate with you through the boys," Farmer suggested.

Understanding the situation completely, Desmond agreed. He first hit him in the head to give him some bruises and then fired a shot through the outer part of Farmer's leg. He then took Farmer's gun and fired it toward the other room so that it looked like he put up a fight. "Quickly get out of here. I will call them so you need to move fast. I will do my best to keep you informed," Farmer winced as he collapsed onto the floor, grabbing one of the discarded towels used as gags to slow the bleeding.

Desmond and Joe bolted out of the patio door following the rest, while Farmer waited a while and dialed Mario's number. "The one who got away last night just shot me. They left a few minutes ago, and I don't know what has happened to Jacqueline," Farmer weakly hollered into the phone and then dropped it as if he passed out. Mario bolted from the table and looked out the window catching sight of the group at a distance heading away from the hotel.

"There they are, quick split up and try to out flank them. Franklin, you follow them while Earl and I try to get ahead of them to cut them off," he ordered, pointing Earl to the left as he took the right. They all took off in a sprint.

Joe didn't see Franklin at first, but it wasn't long before he caught sight of him following them. "Desmond, I am going to engage him if he gets closer you take the rear," he ordered, slowing his pace to create a distance between the battle that would ensue.

Desmond acknowledged and moved on with the group. He did not see Mario coming up on his right until he heard the report of gunfire and the whiz of a bullet just missing him. He dropped and took aim, but because of the ruins did not have a clear shot. "Keep running!" he called to Dalton and Juan who were at the back of the group, as he took cover to engage.

"Run faster, they are shooting at us," Dalton screamed to the adults in the front. Everyone picked up the pace, but not before Earl was able to get close to them.

He did not want to shoot the boys, but he did want to stop them, so he fired a warning shot. Juan looked at Dalton and motioned him toward the ruins to try and distract and confuse their attacker, which it did.

Earl followed the teenagers, thinking that if he caught them the adults would stop. They were just kids, and he knew in his mind he could scare the kids into stopping. He fired again in the direction of the boys and yelled for them to stop.

The boys continued to run and turned in the direction of the Great Ball Court. A large field that was open at both ends, it offered little to no protection. Dalton and Juan knew they could not outrun the gun the man was carrying. As they passed the sign describing the Great Ball Court, Juan spotted the wicker-type ball that was attached to the display. They had seen it on their first visit and had even stopped to read about the court. The Mayans kicked a wicker ball instead of a soccer ball. Dalton reached up and pulled the ball off of the display. He passed it to Juan as he grabbed a stone from the ground thinking that if they did not have bullets they at least had something to use to defend themselves.

As soon as Earl came around the corner into the ball court, Dalton threw the stone, striking him in the chest. When he turned to fire at Dalton, Juan kicked the ball, striking him in the gut, which knocked the wind out of him. Dalton recovered the ball and passed it back to Juan who kicked the ball a second time. It struck Earl in the head and knocked him to the ground.

Out of breath and on his back, Earl realized that he had dropped the gun. He started to rise up to find it just as Dalton used his soccer skills to disable Earl with a wicker ball to the head. Juan swooped in and kicked the gun away. He was comfortable with a machete as he proved in the swamp over the summer, but a gun was a different weapon. Juan ran over to the gun, picked it up, and flung it as far as he could in the trees that surrounded the site. Then both of the boys ran through the court.

Unexpectedly, Earl got up and continued running after them, groggy at first but then alert and angry. He picked up speed with his long legs and began to close in on the teenagers. Juan, out of habit, had kicked the ball on into the court not realizing Earl would come after them again. Juan hollered at Dalton, who ran off to the right to confuse Earl. Earl followed Dalton in hot pursuit and moved within two arms' lengths. Juan slowed his speed and wound up behind them and to the left. Dribbling the ball, he used his right foot to kick the ball hard and low, like a pass, into the back of Earl's knees. It was as if someone had tripped him. Earl fell forward, knees first, and then tumbled multiple times from the momentum. Dalton dodged left and dribbled the ball. Out of pure adrenaline and anger, he sent the ball careening into Earl's head. Juan followed suit with another kick to Earl's head. The wicker ball jarred each time it was kicked and hit its mark. Juan's last kick knocked Earl out cold.

Then Dalton picked up the ball and ran. "Why leave a great ball in the court?" It had saved their lives.

The boys knew where everyone else was heading so they headed that direction.

Meanwhile, Desmond and Mario were in a battle of wits. Both wanted some kind of tactical advantage, but Mario's experience was on the battlefield, whereas Desmond's was urban fighting all over the world. He took to the structures and moved quickly to outflank Mario. Mario was aware of the movement and tried to counter, but he was hemmed in by a high wall, which would expose him for too long if he attempted to climb over it. He continued to follow the contour of the wall, which led him directly into Desmond's line of fire. From his crouched position around a corner, Desmond took aim and pulled the trigger. The bullet pierced Mario's right leg, which made him collapse to the ground. The next shot purposely missed kicking up rocks that sprayed over his body. "Throw your weapons out to the side with your left hand. I fired one warning shot, but the next one will be fatal," Desmond called out from his secure position.

Mario hesitated for a few seconds and realized he had no choice. Changing the gun to this left hand, he threw it hard left. "Now your reserve weapon," demanded Desmond. He was taking no chances, knowing that Mario had been the instigator of this whole ordeal. Again hesitating, but knowing that he had been outsmarted, Mario reached the ankle of his bleeding leg with his left hand, unbuckled the small revolver he kept hidden, and threw it left Then he immediately raised his arms.

Franklin was no match for Joe, whom he was pursuing in the open field. Joe raised his gun and fired two quick shots at the big man. Both bullets hit flesh though they each fell in spots that stopped him but would prove not to be life-threatening. Joe knew that he needed to catch up with the others and get to the safety of the museum security office, so when he saw Franklin crumble to the ground, he turned and resumed his retreat.

Jorge kept everyone else headed in the right direction. Steve stayed with him, but given all of the excitement and gunfire, Jorge had not looked back to see that Juan and Dalton were no longer with them. He was told to keep moving so people would know where to go. With Ramón, Peter, and Mercedes close by and Steve beside him, Jorge missed all of the action. As soon as he reached the museum security office door, he began to scream *"Ayuda!"* getting the attention of the two guards in the control room. When one of them bolted through the door, he was taken aback to see a man with a drawn gun and others piling in behind him.

"Help, there are men with guns following us and shooting at us!" he screamed in Spanish as the guard began to draw his own weapon.

"I am their protection," Steve announced quickly as to not be shot by the museum guard. "There are others out there trying to get in and at least three bad guys with guns. Call your boss to let him know what's going on and see if you can track the others with your cameras. I will cover the door."

The security guard turned quickly back to the control room and called his boss to alert all the guards on duty at the complex. Then he directed the other guard to pull up cameras and watch for the intruders and victims. The screens were already up, but he focused his search on cameras that were nearby. Jorge had moved in to help them identify the perpetrators and was shocked when he saw what was happening in the Great Ball Court.

"That's my son and his best friend!" he screamed, pointing at the screen in the top row far right. They watched in horror as the man moved in close to catch Juan and Dalton. Their gasps of horror turned to laughter as they watched Juan knock the big guy down with whatever they were kicking and then as each boy took turns passing and shooting the object into the head of the guy until he quit moving. Jorge and the guard realized that it was a ball of some sort as they watched the boys pick it up and run away from the unconscious man. The head security guard sent one of his men who was close to detain the guy on the ground, which wasn't difficult since he was unconscious.

They moved their attention to another screen where they saw another man lying on the ground. "That's one of them also," exhaled Jorge, pointing now to a screen in the middle. The view focused on a man sprawled out in the dirt. Jorge could identify the man as Franklin, the one who had been in hot pursuit, but he could not see Joe, who was to cover from behind. Along with guards, museum security ordered an ambulance to the site as well.

The last person they could see on the screens was Desmond holding Mario at gunpoint. "Who is that?" the security chief asked.

"That is Desmond holding the last bad guy. Do you have someone else to send?" Jorge asked.

Immediately, he got on the radio and called the last security guard on duty, the one standing in the lobby with Mercedes, Peter, and Ramón. He sent him toward Desmond, giving him orders to go and take the man on the ground into custody. "Are there any more gunmen?" the guard inquired.

"No, there are two others, but they are back at the hotel, one with a bullet in the leg and the other a woman, but they were not aggressive," replied Jorge.

As he spoke, the boys came through the front door laughing. Jorge ran out into the lobby where everyone else was and wrapped his arms around Juan, nearly crushing him. "Don't think we didn't see what you did back there," his father chided. "We saw you both being chased in the ball court and then you knocking him down with the ball. We also saw your shots at the guy, Dalton. I guess all of the soccer practice paid off, but not quite like we expected," he laughed, letting go of Juan and turning and hugging Dalton. He never expected to see his "boys" take on a guy with a gun.

Soon Desmond opened the door and everyone sighed a sigh of relief. Everyone was safe and protected and all of the bad guys were in custody and heading to the local hospital. Ramón turned to the group, "I am not used to this kind of action, I sit at a desk or dig in the dirt all day."

Dalton laughed, "Juan and I are getting used to it. It's like everywhere we go people are wanting to shoot us, and they're not even our teachers over grades!"

Chapter 13

Returning from the Underworld

S ecurity called the Mexican federal police to come and take custody of the three men as they lay recuperating in the hospital. Since it happened at an archaeological site, they had jurisdiction. It also helped that a federal employee had been kidnapped.

Desmond and the boys went to the hospital to check on James Farmer since Desmond shot him in the leg. Because it had been a clean shot that did not hit anything major, the doctors were able to stitch him up but wanted to keep him in the hospital overnight because he had lost a lot of blood. The federal police were going to arrest Farmer and Dr. Montavilla for their participation, but Ramón explained that they were unaware of the kidnapping plot and had actually helped with the escape. After questioning them, each was free to go.

"I am sorry I shot you," Desmond apologized.

"You just shot me because I beat you up in Santo Domingo," he laughed.

Desmond and Farmer chatted a while longer and then drove Dr. Montavilla back to her hotel. On the way, the three of them talked about the discovery. "Are you going to go back in and get it?" Dr. Montavilla inquired.

"That is up to Ramón. Technically, the find belongs to the site, so it's their decision as to whether it stays where it is or goes on display. I think it would be safer to bring it out because we already know what people will do to try and get at it," Desmond answered. "What are your intentions?"

"Mr. Lanning paid me to find the source of the gold, and if my hunch is right we found it. I do not wish to do anything else with him after he hired Mario and how all of that turned out."

"If we go back in, Mercedes will go this time since you took her place. I am sure she would be willing to go over the photos that Ramón took and you can help sort them out, but that is up to her because she is our archaeologist," informed Desmond.

"That seems fair, especially since you didn't press charges on me. I will ask her and Ramón when we get back.'

After dropping her at the hotel, Desmond and the boys went back to the museum security office and found Steve, Joe, Ramón, Peter, Mercedes, and Jorge recovering from the days ordeal. "Steve and Joe, thank you so much for coming and saving us. I know that you did it for Mr. Swartz, but I am in your debt," said Desmond. "What are your plans now?"

"If it is all right with you guys, we want to stick around. Ramón and Mercedes were just talking about getting the statue out. We thought that would be cool. And since it appears to be valuable, we can provide protection for you," Steve replied.

The SMU team all agreed, but they were tired so they headed back to Jorge's parents' house while Steve and Joe checked in at the hotel. It had been a long and tiring night, so they decided to meet at 10:00 p.m. to go to the cenote and retrieve the statue.

As evening approached, the SMU team, James Farmer, and Dr. Montavilla met at the cenote. Farmer convinced the hospital he was well enough to go and left on crutches. He had heard that the SMU team was going to retrieve the statue and he wanted to be present when they did. Even Steve and Joe showed up to provide support and protection, which was unnecessary since Ramón had requested that the federal police be there. Everyone pitched in to carry the scuba tanks, equipment, and submersible down the steps.

Dalton and Juan helped Peter set up the submersible and launch it. Dalton found the safety line he left the night before and got in place to help. Ramón, Mercedes, and Desmond donned their scuba gear after each had checked it for safety. Ramón had previously downloaded the pictures that he took, so while everyone was preparing, Dr. Montavilla was going through them seeing if anything was missed or there was something significant they needed more pictures of while inside the inner pyramid. She and Ramón discussed what pictures needed to be retaken and a couple of areas that she knew were missed, and he made note of it. They both doubted that anyone would enter the inner pyramid again so they wanted to document it completely for further study.

Desmond slipped below the water first, followed by Mercedes, and then Ramón. The guys did not carry extra tanks for emergencies since there were spares already there. Instead of a ladder, Mercedes carried a collapsible litter that emergency responders use to carry hurt people. It was decided that the litter along with some blow-up flotation devices could be rigged to carry the statue out at neutral buoyancy so that it would hover in the water not going up or down. With the statue on the flotation device, they could push it along instead of lifting it. It was the same principle that the BC vests used to allow them to float at whatever depth they chose.

Peter led the group with the submersible since the life line was already in place, using his bright light and prerecorded dive plan to guide them. Desmond, Mercedes, and Ramón followed the submersible, stopping only to check the tanks that were previously left. After twenty minutes, the three of them arrived in the entrance to the inner pyramid. They ascended the ladder that had been left after removing their diving gear. Desmond, being the last out, gave a thumbs-up to Peter through the camera.

Mercedes had seen the pictures that had been taken, but she was astounded to see the site for herself in person. She splayed her light over every wall, stopping at each drawing and carving to take her own pictures. Everyone agreed that they would take their time so no one hurried her as she lingered taking pictures. Ramón directed her to the areas that Dr.

Montavilla thought needed better shots and those areas they had missed. Mercedes used her knowledge of Mayan hieroglyphs to meticulously put each in order as she took them. She knew she was reading a story on the walls and made certain she started at the beginning.

While Mercedes chronicled the frescos, Ramón and Desmond worked on moving the statue. They first assembled the litter inside the circle that stood in front of the statue. They had expanded the litter so that the statue would fit. Ramón had estimated the weight to be little more than two hundred pounds. But as he began tipping it, he found that it was lighter than that. Ramón grabbed one end and Desmond the other, and they gently placed the statue in the litter. Desmond used straps to tie the statue to the litter and then attached the air bags that would be filled once it was in the water.

As Mercedes finished her work, she climbed down the ladder and donned her scuba tank. Her job was to fill the air bags halfway at first and then add more air once the litter with the statue was in the water so that it would have neutral buoyancy. The men were tasked with climbing down the ladder with the litter and statue. Ramón went first while Desmond tied another rope to the litter and secured it around the pillar. Desmond used his strength and weight as a counterbalance as he slowly payed out the line, lowering the statue to Ramón. As it reached the water, Mercedes filled the first of the air bladders half full and then as the other end reached the water she filled the other bladder.

With the rope still attached, Ramón donned his scuba tank and help slide the litter farther into the water. As it began to sink, Mercedes hurriedly blew up the bladders until the statue was no longer sinking but was not rising either, neutral buoyancy. Desmond also untied the collapsible ladder and carried it into the water, deciding to make it more difficult for anyone who returned. Mercedes understood as Desmond tied it to her tank.

While all of this was going on, Ramón had attached the guide rope to the submersible. Their plan was to go out as they first came in, with the submersible holding the line tight until they were back at the entrance to the cenote. Peter would bring the rope out as Dalton and Juan pulled in the extra tanks. The system worked as planned. The only problem they encountered was having to adjust the air bags along the way to fit through the holes. When they arrived at the cenote opening, Desmond and Ramón took each end of the litter and filled their own BC vests with air while Mercedes filled the air bladders to full, causing it to rise. Cheers went up the moment it broke water.

Steve and Joe threw lines to the men in the water, who tied them to the litter. They pulled it to the edge and with everyone's help were able to lift it out of the water. They set it on the ground and immediately began taking pictures of all of them and the statue.

Peter, Dalton, and Juan pulled in the remaining line and tanks and cleared everything out of the water. They didn't want to leave any of their equipment and most of all the submersible. Once everything was stowed away, they stood up the statue, still attached to the litter, and gathered around for a picture. Farmer happily took it since he was only a spectator to all of it. There sitting on each side of the statue of Yum Cimil were Dalton and Juan with Desmond and Mercedes and Jorge to the right, Ramón and Jacqueline to the left and Peter, with his submersible. They had quite the celebration as they laughed and joked about being kidnapped and finding the prince of the underworld.

They carried the statue up to a waiting truck, that would take it to the museum where it would be locked up in a vault to be studied by Ramón and others in the future. Before Steve and Joe headed back to the hotel, they visited with Desmond, debriefing everything that happened and exchanging phone numbers. They realized that they had a lot in common and agreed to get together once they were back in the States.

Before leaving, Ramón had each person, including Dr. Montavilla, sign a nondisclosure statement to keep anyone from talking about the find publicly until Ramón and the National Institute of Anthropology and History issued an official release. Ramón wanted to make certain that they could protect the statue and the inner pyramid from future entry.

Jorge drove Juan, Dalton, Mercedes, Desmond, and Peter back to his parents' house for a good night's rest and then off to the airport early the next morning, which was Sunday. With all the excitement going on, everyone had forgotten that the boys had to go back to school on Monday.

The SMU team flew home the next morning, as did Peter, Farmer, and Dr. Montavilla. Mario, Earl, and Franklin remained, recuperating in the hospital and then off to a Mexican prison to await trial for kidnapping. Farmer and Dr. Montavilla met with Mr. Lanning after they arrived. Both accused him of trying to kill them by hiring Mario Franklin, and Earl, and each demanded a severance package and immediately left his employment. Once again, Mr. Lanning had been beaten by two teenage boys and their people. Dr. Montavilla went back to lecturing in a college, and Farmer went home to recover from his wound. He contemplated retiring, but he received a phone call offering him an assignment that seemed interesting.

Epilogue

The boys returned to school on Monday, excited but tired from their week. Molly found Dalton before school started. "How did your trip to Mexico go?" she asked.

"You are not going to like my answer, but I can't tell you right now. We signed papers that said we couldn't talk about it for a couple of months, but just so you will know we had an exciting adventure that you are not going to believe," Dalton answered with a wide grin on his face. That was not what she wanted to hear and that was not what Dalton wanted to tell his new girlfriend. He almost slipped several times as they visited, but she stopped him, not wanting him to get in trouble. When anyone else asked about their Thanksgiving break, they told them they went to Mexico and visited Juan's grandparents.

Two months later, they got an e-mail from Ramón telling them that the next day the National Institute of Anthropology and History was releasing the story and photos so the world would know what happened in Mexico. Dalton and Juan could finally tell their friends about their adventure. Dalton called Molly immediately and said, "Let's meet, I can officially tell you about our find!"

Molly ran to find her mother, who was very curious herself by now, and she agreed to drive them to McDonald's where Dalton pulled out pictures and diagrams and even some of the research he had found. He showed Molly the pictures of the ruins, the pictures of the cenote and even pictures from the cave. He also told her about the gold statue and being kidnapped and how Desmond and two other men helped them escape. As Molly sat there listening to his story, tears began to flow down her cheeks. Those tears turned to laughter when Dalton talked about how he and Juan escaped by kicking a wicker ball at a gunman.

"You just made that last part up just to scare me, didn't you?" she whimpered.

"Thinking back on it, I wish I had made it up, but it was true. It all happened so fast, we just did what we knew how to do to save our lives," Dalton quietly said, holding her now trembling hands. "The security guards gave us a video of what their cameras had captured," he said, turning his phone toward her with it playing. She quit crying and began to laugh, because as dangerous as it was it looked more like a crazy movie of kids playing.

When Molly got home, she shared the story with her mom. Doubting the account, her mom called Dr. Miller, who verified everything in Dalton's story and then she sat in wonder at this amazing young man who was dating her daughter.

Mercedes returned to SMU and was able to continue researching the pictures that she had taken. She cooperated with Ramón and the National Institute of Anthropology and History by translating the story from the temple and co-authored the paper that Ramón and the institute released. She finally received recognition for her work and SMU allowed her to use the paper for her doctoral thesis. She also began seeing Desmond socially when he was in town, which seemed to be less each month. She didn't know where he was going, but after he met up with Steve and Joe, they formed a partnership and began working together. He did not talk much about his work, but it kept him from finishing his studies.

Peter, upon release of the story, was able to use their discovery to promote OpenRov and the submersible. He was promoted to vice president of the company and was often asked to speak at events about the use of submersibles. He also looked back over the pictures he took in the cave, especially the ones of the unusual floor of the cave. What he thought were just bumps in the bottom turned out to be the bones of people dumped into the cenote. He could clearly see skulls and skeletons littering the bottom in the mud. His discovery proved human sacrifices had been made to Yum Cimil and that the bodies were dumped into the cenote.

Mercedes final translation of the hieroglyphs told the story of how the original builders of the inner pyramid worshipped Yum Cimil and appeased him with their human offerings. It also told of the gold mines that the Mayans discovered not far from the site and the things that were made for worship there, some of which were found on *El Dorado*, tying it to Chichén Itzá. The gold mines were known by the National Institute of Anthropology and History but had played out hundreds of years ago. So, everything Mr. Lanning had set out to discover and take had been found and it all came to a dead end in the empty mines, other than the statue of Yum Cimil on sight.

www.ingramcontent.com/pod-product-compliance
Lightning Source LLC
Chambersburg PA
CBHW050952120626
46552CB00001B/503